PRAISE FOR

"In the tradition of LaVyrle Spencer, gifted author Barbara Freethy creates an irresistible tale of family secrets, riveting adventure and heart- touching romance."

*-- NYT Bestselling Author **Susan Wiggs***
on Summer Secrets

"This book has it all: heart, community, and characters who will remain with you long after the book has ended. A wonderful story."

*-- NYT Bestselling Author **Debbie Macomber***
on Suddenly One Summer

"Freethy has a gift for creating complex characters."

*-- **Library Journal***

"Barbara Freethy is a master storyteller with a gift for spinning tales about ordinary people in extraordinary situations and drawing readers into their lives."

*-- **Romance Reviews Today***

"Freethy's skillful plotting and gift for creating sympathetic characters will ensure that few dry eyes will be left at the end of the story."

*-- **Publishers Weekly** on The Way Back Home*

"Freethy skillfully keeps the reader on the hook, and her tantalizing and believable tale has it all-- romance, adventure, and mystery."

*-- **Booklist** on Summer Secrets*

"Freethy's story-telling ability is top-notch."

*-- **Romantic Times** on Don't Say A Word*

Also Available

7 Brides for 7 Soldiers Series

Other Popular Novels by Barbara Freethy

RYDER

7 Brides for 7 Soldiers, #1

BARBARA FREETHY

HYDE
STREET
—PRESS—

HYDE STREET PRESS
Published by Hyde Street Press
1325 Howard Avenue, #321
Burlingame, California 94010

Printed in the United States of America

Cover design by Damonza.com

ISBN: 978-1-944417-34-5

Prologue

—➤➤◄◄←—

"We're hit! We're hit!"

Navy pilot Ryder Westbrook heard the panicked words of his copilot, Michael Valdez, but he was too busy trying to regain control of the SH-60 Seahawk helicopter to reply. They were coming back from a humanitarian mission—having dropped food, water and medical supplies into the rugged and remote villages of Afghanistan—when they'd taken enemy fire.

They weren't going to make it back to the carrier in the Persian Gulf. They were going to have to set down somewhere, hopefully far from the rebel forces that had just shot at them.

His heart pounded against his chest, but he remained calm, his training playing through his head as he went through every option to retain control of the twin-engine helicopter.

Flying was in his blood. The helo had always felt like an extension of his own power, but now that power was crumbling, and he was being forcibly reminded of just how fragile life could be.

But he couldn't quit. There had to be a way out.

Unfortunately, his optimism was dampened by the fact that the ground was getting closer by the second, and his crew was depending on him to get them down safely.

His copilot had a wife and a baby back in the States. Colin Forbes, the sensor operator, was getting married in a month. And he…well, he still had things he wanted to do.

He had to keep them all alive.

Searching the ground for a viable landing site, he spotted what appeared to be a flat, open rural area. Not only did he want to protect his crew, he didn't want to hurt anyone on the ground.

Glancing over at Michael, he saw his friend making the sign of the cross.

"We're not going to die," he said emphatically, drawing Michael's gaze to his. "Not today. Not this time."

He could see the hope in Michael's eyes. His friend wanted to believe him.

Hell, he wanted to believe himself.

He'd been in tight spots before, and he'd always come out on top. It had been that way his entire life. Growing up in Eagle's Ridge, he'd been the golden boy—the one who set new records, who made things happen, who achieved whatever he went after.

But this was real life. This was happening now, and he was the only one who could save all their lives.

In ten years of naval service, he'd never encountered a situation exactly like this. He'd never felt so worried that his number might really be up.

He shook the negative thought out of his head, squaring his jaw, tightening his hand on the controls, as he rode the bird down to the ground.

The impact was harder than he'd expected, the helicopter shattering into pieces of fiery metal. And when everything went black, he fought against the idea that this might be it.

He had more he wanted to do, people he should have made peace with a long time ago, a home that beckoned to him—the Blue Mountains, the Snake River, the people of Eagle's Ridge—a life still to be lived.

He needed more time… He just didn't know if he was going to get it.

One

⟶⟫⟪⟵

"I just need some time," Bailey Tucker said, her hand tightening around her phone as her good friend, Shannon Cooper, asked her for the third time why she'd left New York in the dead of the night without so much as a conversation. "I need things to die down," she added, still cringing at how stupid she'd been.

She sat down at the table in her father's kitchen, looking around a room that was comfortably familiar but also an uncomfortable reminder of her latest failure.

She'd left this house eight years ago at the age of twenty. She'd gone to the local community college after high school. Then she'd moved to New York to attend culinary school. Classes and jobs in Paris and Rome had followed, and eventually she'd returned to the Big Apple to work for a brilliant chef and to hopefully take her career to new heights. But this week everything had shattered—her professional life and her personal life.

Now she was hiding out and licking her wounds

in Eagle's Ridge, a small town in southeastern Washington State, shadowed by the Blue Mountains and nourished by the Snake River, a place she loved but was about as far from her dreams as she could possibly be.

She couldn't imagine what everyone would think about her shameful return. She could now consider herself a joke on both coasts.

"Franco should have been the one to leave town, not you," Shannon said, the anger in her voice drawing Bailey back to the conversation. "Nothing that happened was your fault."

"According to Franco, it was all my fault. You saw what happened when I tried to defend myself—he made it all worse. He said things about me—" She stopped abruptly, unable to say the words aloud. "I can't even bear to repeat them."

"Everything he said was a lie."

"It doesn't matter. He has more credibility than I do."

"I don't think that's true. You just haven't had the same opportunity to tell your side of the story. That's why you need to come back."

"I can't," she said. "I've tried to talk to the press, but they are all on Franco's side. He's a celebrity in the culinary world. No one wants to believe anything but the best about him, and he's incredibly good at spinning lies. I just can't be in the city right now. As soon as we end this call, I am going to toss my phone into the river, because I am being blasted by texts."

"They can't be all bad. You have friends."

"Some people are supportive, but the pity is almost as bad as everything else."

"It will blow over. I know it's big news in the

foodie world, but there are a lot of people in Manhattan who have never heard of you or Franco," Shannon pointed out.

"You're right, but the only thing that felt good in the last seven days was getting on a plane and coming home."

"You always told me that Eagle's Ridge was too small for you, that you had bigger dreams."

"Well, those dreams turned into nightmares. And right now, Eagle's Ridge feels safe. My dad is here, my grandpa, my older brothers Adam and Zane. They're both out of the service now. It's odd that for a long time we were all gone, and now we're back in the same place again."

"Have you told your family what happened?"

"Not yet. When I arrived late last night, I just saw my dad, and I said that I needed a break, that I was missing home. He didn't ask a lot of questions, which is pretty much the way he is. He said we'd talk when I was ready, which might be never. I just don't want to disappoint everyone. I left with big proclamations a long time ago about how I was going to change the culinary world, and I certainly haven't done that." She felt a little embarrassed at the memory of how cocky her twenty-year-old-self had been.

"I'm sure your family will understand."

"Maybe, but my brothers have done big things. Zane was an Army cavalry scout. Adam was a Coast Guard rescue swimmer. They both literally saved people. They followed the tradition of service fostered in this town, and I didn't. I just wanted to cook."

"Hey, people have to eat. Cooking is important."

She smiled at Shannon's pragmatic comment. "Thanks for that."

"So, what did you do today?"

"Nothing. I wasn't quite ready to venture outside. My brother Zane stopped by briefly. He was in a hurry so he said we'd talk later. His main purpose for coming by was to ask my dad to watch his dog tonight, because apparently his floors are being redone. Since my father is going to be out, I volunteered. And, if you can believe it, I actually had to beg for the dog-sitting job."

"You did not."

"I did. Zane doesn't think I'm very good with animals, because one time while I was watching his goldfish while he was at camp, it died. Like that was my fault."

"Definitely not your fault."

"And apparently his dog Gambler has a long list of things he doesn't like. I haven't read the entire list yet, but I think doorbells and bubble wrapping were at the top." She glanced at the large clock on the kitchen wall. It was almost seven. "I should probably get Gambler some food. I wonder why he hasn't been bugging me." Uneasiness suddenly ran through her. She hadn't actually seen Gambler since Shannon had called.

"Hang on—are you good with animals, Bailey?" Shannon asked doubtfully. "Didn't you *not* date that guy from Brooklyn because he had two cats?"

"It wasn't the cats that I didn't like; it was the way he talked to them, like they were his girlfriends. It gave me the creeps." A cool breeze lifted her hair, and she shivered, wondering why it was suddenly colder.

Frowning, she got up, walked down the hall and saw that the front door was open.

Her heart leapt into her chest. "Oh, no!" She put

her hand over the phone and yelled, "Gambler!" No response. "I have to go, Shannon."

"What's wrong?"

"Gambler escaped."

"No way."

"I cannot lose Zane's dog. He will never forgive me. And can this week get any worse—seriously?"

"Go. Call me later. And don't throw your phone in the river."

"I can't make any promises."

She ended the call, slipped her phone into her pocket and ran out the front door. Her father's house was in the woods, with the nearest neighbor—her grandfather—almost two miles away. It wasn't like Gambler could run into traffic, but there was plenty of wildlife in the area, not to mention the river about two hundred yards away.

"Gambler," she yelled again. "It's dinner time. Aren't you hungry?" She ran through the brush, her feet slipping on the wet leaves and muddy ground. Apparently, the first two weeks of March had been very rainy.

Her brothers would be happy about that. The more rain, the higher and faster the river ran, perfect for their adventure watersports business. Unfortunately, it was not perfect for running in the woods in flats better suited for a city street in Manhattan.

"Gambler," she called out again, pausing as she heard barking.

Following the sound, she ended up in a marshy meadow that had turned into a wet tributary with the nearby river spilling over its banks.

Gambler had somehow managed to get himself

onto a tiny island of dirt about ten yards away from her. He was barking and looking at the water and then looking at her.

"Come on, boy," she said, patting her thighs as she urged him to come back.

Gambler barked in response. He put one paw in the water, then backed out.

"If you don't like the water, how did you get out there?" she asked.

Gambler backed up, barking again. She suddenly realized what was upsetting him when she saw several splashes in the water near him, along with the sound of frogs.

Frogs! Dammit! Frogs were on the list of things Gambler didn't like, weren't they?

She vaguely remembered seeing them on the list, and she probably should have paid more attention, but she hadn't planned on Gambler getting out of the house. In fact, she still didn't know how he'd accomplished that. She was one hundred percent sure she'd locked the front door.

Well, maybe eighty percent sure...

She'd opened the door when a package had arrived for her father, and she'd chatted maybe a minute with the delivery man, who was a longtime friend of the family. But she thought she'd closed the door when he left.

She sighed. It didn't really matter at this point. What did matter was getting Gambler into the house and dried off before Zane came back.

"Gambler, come on, boy. You can do it," she said again. "I'll give you a treat."

Gambler barked, then roamed around his tiny island, before barking again.

Putting her hands on her hips, she assessed the situation. It didn't look like Gambler was running back through the water to join her any time soon. That meant she needed to go and get him, but wading through the muddy, cold water wasn't high on her list of things to do. Still, she had no choice. It was a standoff, and Gambler was winning.

"Okay, fine," she muttered. "It's not like you're the first male to want everything his own way."

She looked down at her flats, debating on going barefoot or using them to protect her feet against the rocky ground. She decided to go for protection after seeing a layer of mud already piled on each shoe. They were done for anyway. She rolled up her jeans to her knees and then waded into the water. It was slow going, her feet sinking deep into the wet ground, the water swirling around her calves and knees, and by the time she reached Gambler's tiny sanctuary island, she was feeling wet and cold.

She grabbed Gambler's collar and tried to pull him toward her, but he was ninety-pounds of terrified dog, and he wasn't budging.

"Come on, the frogs are not going to hurt you," she pleaded. "I'll protect you."

She tried pulling him toward the water once again, but he reared back so abruptly, she was knocked off her feet. She let out a scream as she landed hard on her ass in the water.

Could her life get any worse? And then she realized it could when a frog jumped onto her head. She scrambled to her feet, trying to get the frog out of her now wet, tangled hair.

"Hey," a man shouted, waving to her. "Are you all right?"

She finally knocked the frog back into the water and then turned her gaze toward the man standing on the bank. He looked familiar, wearing jeans and a black leather jacket over a dark T-shirt. In the evening shadows, she couldn't see his features clearly, but the sound of his voice had taken her back in time. She pushed strands of hair away from her eyes. "Ryder Westbrook?"

"Yes, and you are…"

He didn't recognize her?

Well, of course he wouldn't. Why would he? Ryder Westbrook was four years older than her, and he'd been the golden boy of Eagle's Ridge—the high school quarterback, the basketball all-star, the class president, following in a long line of Westbrooks who thought they owned the town. His girlfriends had all been beautiful and all had come from the other side of the river, the wealthy side—the side the Westbrooks had stolen from her family sixty-five years ago.

"What's your name?" he asked.

"Bailey Tucker." She couldn't keep the irritation out of her voice.

"Adam and Zane's little sister?" he asked in surprise.

"That would be me."

"You need some help?"

She jumped back as a frog landed on her foot. She kicked it into the water while Gambler barked again. "Does it look like I need help?"

"It does," he said, amusement in his voice. "What are you doing out there?"

"I'm rescuing Zane's dog."

"He looks fine to me."

"Oh, he's fine all right—he's just nuts. He's scared

of frogs."

"How did he get out there?"

"I have no idea. He ran away from the house, and I found him here." She looked down at the dog, who was nuzzling her hand and now seemed happy to have her with him on the island. "Oh, sure, now you want to make friends, Gambler. You just knocked me off my feet."

"Gambler?" Ryder echoed. "Your brother's dog is named Gambler? That's fitting."

Since Zane's love of betting was well known in Eagle's Ridge, she couldn't argue with that. "Yes, and you can go. We're fine."

"You're fine? How are you getting Gambler through those frog-infested waters?"

"I'm thinking about carrying him."

"He looks like he weighs more than you do."

"Yes, well, it will work out. Don't worry about it." She didn't need Ryder Westbrook witnessing her latest disastrous moment.

"I could help you," he offered.

"I don't think so."

"Why not?"

"Because…"

"Because I'm a man and you're an independent woman?" he challenged.

"No, because you're a Westbrook and I'm a Tucker," she snapped back. "Tuckers don't get help from Westbrooks."

Good grief! Where had that come from? She was channeling her grandfather's favorite mantra.

"Seriously?" Ryder asked. "You're bringing up that old feud?"

"If you spent five minutes with my grandfather,

you'll know it's as fresh in his mind now as it was when it started sixty-five years ago."

"Well, it's fresh in my grandfather's mind, too, but we're not them. And if you don't accept my help, you're going to have to leave Gambler and go find one of your brothers. Then who knows what will happen to the dog?"

He made a really good point. The last thing she wanted was for Zane to find out she'd let Gambler out of the house.

Taking favors from a Westbrook went against the grain, but there was a part of her that thought it was a silly old feud, too. Besides that, she was getting cold covered in muddy river water. And there was no way she could carry Gambler back to the shore.

Before she could say anything, Ryder was making his way toward her, striding through the foot-deep water with steadier feet and a hell of a lot more purpose than she had.

He looked a bit like a rugged, powerful warrior, and a shiver ran down her spine that had nothing to do with the chill in her bones.

It was possible she might have had a tiny crush on him when she was younger—really tiny—barely there.

As Ryder got closer, the moonlight danced off the planes of his handsome face, and she swallowed a knot in her throat.

Okay, so he was even better looking than he'd been in high school. So what?

She was off men forever, or at least the foreseeable future. And even if she wasn't off men— Ryder Westbrook would definitely be off-limits. He was a Westbrook and she was a Tucker, and if there was anyone in the world she owed loyalty to, it was her grandfather.

But when Ryder reached her, she felt even more overwhelmed by his attractiveness. Up close, the power of his body, the breadth of his shoulders, the sexiness of his mouth, the hint of humor in his eyes sent little trills down her spine. And she couldn't help but wish she didn't look a little better than a bedraggled, soppy mess.

"Hey, buddy," he said to the dog.

Gambler was happy to meet a new friend and immediately jumped up, putting his muddy paws on Ryder's chest.

To his credit, Ryder didn't take offense at the new layer of mud on his jacket. Instead, he took the opportunity to swoop Gambler up in his arms. The ninety-pound dog tried to wrangle free, but Ryder was having none of that. "Stop," he said in an authoritative voice. "You're fine."

Somehow Gambler seemed to believe him, quieting his panicked movements.

She watched in astonishment as Ryder carried Gambler back through the frog-filled marsh and set him down on dry land. Gambler barked and then lay down, as if exhausted by his adventure.

She was torn between relief that Gambler was safe and annoyance that Ryder Westbrook had saved the day. But that was petty. All that mattered was that she had not lost Zane's dog in the river.

"You need some help?" Ryder called back to her. "Want me to carry you?"

"Not a chance," she said, stepping into the cold water. She waded back to the shore, stumbling a few times as her feet sank into the mud. When she got close, Ryder extended his hand.

She hesitated for one minute, not really sure why. She told herself it was because of the feud between their grandparents, but she didn't really think that was it.

There was just something about taking Ryder's hand that seemed dangerous...like she was crossing a line she shouldn't cross.

"Really?" he asked dryly. "You're as stubborn as your grandfather, Bailey."

"I'll take that as a compliment."

"It wasn't meant as one."

"I know." She tried to take another step, but the mud sucked her foot down deeper into the ground, and she almost fell over. She might be stubborn, but she wasn't completely stupid. She grabbed Ryder's hand.

His strong fingers closed over hers, and he pulled her onto dry land.

"Okay?" he asked, his gaze sweeping across her face.

She nodded, her mouth going dry as his eyes met hers. "I'm fine." She belatedly let go of his hand. "Thanks."

"No problem."

"What were you doing out here anyway?" she asked. The only two houses on this stretch of road belonged to her father and grandfather.

"I stopped at your dad's house. I wanted to talk to him about some business I'd like to do with your grandfather. I heard barking and yelling and decided to investigate."

She was confused by his words. "You have business with my grandfather? I can't imagine what that could be."

"I have a proposition for him."

"No. You have a death wish. My grandfather hates everyone with your last name."

"I'm aware of that, which is why I wanted to reach out to your father first. This could be a very viable financial venture for your family."

"If that venture is tied to your family, my grandpa will not be interested."

"Wouldn't he be interested in bringing more business and more tourists to Eagle's Ridge?"

Her gaze narrowed. "Aren't you in the Navy, Ryder? What's this all about?"

"I was in the Navy. I'm not anymore."

"Why not?"

"It doesn't matter. I got out a few weeks ago. Now, I'm taking over operations at the Eagle's Ridge Airfield, and I'd like to lengthen one of the runways so we can bring in bigger planes. It will be better for tourism as well as for aircraft participating in search and rescue, fire assault, etc. All I need is a few more acres of land."

Now, she knew where he was going... "Tucker land."

He nodded. "Yes."

"But the city owns the airport, doesn't it? Why isn't the mayor or the city council talking to my grandfather?"

"Because the city doesn't have the money in the budget this year for that kind of purchase. They said it could be five years before they could raise the cash. But if I buy the land now, I can get started on my plans, and eventually the city will buy it back from me." He paused. "I have considered the possibility that your grandfather might be more willing to sell to the city than to me, but it's a long time to wait. We need the expansion now."

"Your family is fairly synonymous with the city; I'm not sure it would make a difference, especially if you're the one running the airport. Which brings me to another question—what happened to David Bennett— to his son Greg? I thought they ran the airport."

"Greg is retiring. The Bennetts are done with running the airport."

"Did you ask David to ask my grandfather? They're very close friends."

"David says he can't or won't do it. That he made it a rule a long time ago not to take sides between Westbrooks and Tuckers. So, it's on me."

She folded her arms across her chest, studying his intense expression. There was a willful purpose in his eyes that told her he wasn't going to take no for an answer—at least not without a fight. There were also shadows in his gaze, and she couldn't help wondering what the story was behind his leaving the service. Ryder had gone to the Naval Academy right out of high school. He'd had, according to her brothers, an illustrious and meritorious naval career, risking his life more than once to save others.

"Why did you leave the Navy?" she asked.

He shrugged. "It was time."

"That's vague."

"Is it? There's no big story. I just decided to do something else."

She wasn't quite sure she believed that, but Ryder obviously wasn't interested in giving her more information.

Gambler got up and started barking, obviously now rested and hungry. "I have to get Gambler back to the house."

"Okay." Ryder fell into step alongside her.

"My father isn't home tonight," she added. "He's playing cards with my grandfather and some family friends. But it doesn't matter that they're not here for you to talk to. My grandfather will not sell his land to you, not one inch of it. You're a Westbrook. He won't see past that, especially not when it comes to land. He believes your family stole the best land in this area right out from under him. You already know that."

"I know it's an old fight that should have ended a long time ago."

"That might be true, but that's not the way my grandfather will see it."

"I can be fairly persuasive."

"Maybe with the ladies, but Max Tucker is another story."

"We'll see." He gave her a curious look. "When did you get back to town, Bailey? I thought you were living in New York these days, cooking at some super fancy restaurant."

She sucked in a breath, hoping he hadn't heard more than that. "I was doing that. I got in last night."

"For a visit, or…"

"I don't know yet. I'm exploring my options."

"That sounds like the beginning of a story."

"Your leaving the Navy sounds like a better one," she returned. "I thought you were going to be a lifer."

"Things change."

"Yes, they do," she muttered.

"Maybe we'll share our stories some time."

"I doubt that. You're on the wrong side of the river, Ryder."

"Your brothers don't hate me because of my last

name—why do you? Habit? Family tradition? Or is there another reason?" he queried.

"I don't hate you. I just don't think we have anything to talk about. But thanks for helping me with Gambler." She paused at the bottom of the steps leading up to her dad's house. "The feud goes two ways, Ryder. If you want to end the fight, why not start with your family? Why not talk to your grandfather?"

"He doesn't own the land in question, so talking to him can't help me."

"It might help you understand that the hatred between our families goes back a long time. If anyone is going to end this feud, it will probably have to be the men who started it."

"Maybe not. Maybe it's up to us, to our generation."

"Have you spoken to Adam or Zane about your quest to get the land?"

"I spoke briefly to Zane. He told me he wouldn't bet on my success."

"That should tell you something," she said dryly. "Because Zane will bet on just about anything."

A smile curved his lips. "I know that. His bets got me into trouble back in the day."

"I'm sure you're used to getting your way, Ryder, but I think you've met your match in my grandfather."

"Then maybe you should help me," he suggested.

"I don't think so. I have enough of my own problems."

"Just think about it."

"I don't want to waste my time. There's no way in hell my grandfather will sell you his land."

"I can't take no for an answer."

"Then you better not ask the question." Pausing, she added. "Do you want to come in and clean up before you get in your truck?"

"I'm fine."

"Okay. Thanks for your help."

"You're welcome. I'll see you around."

"Maybe," she said vaguely. She kicked off her shoes and rolled up her jeans, then opened the front door and let Gambler into the house. He'd leave some muddy footprints, but right now she just wanted to get inside. Gambler immediately bounded down the hall toward the kitchen, obviously looking for dinner.

She closed the door behind her and let out a breath. Impulsively, she moved into the living room and looked out the window, watching as Ryder got into his Jeep. More tingles ran down her spine. She liked confidence, men who had ambition, drive, even stubbornness. But she could not *like* Ryder; that would be a mistake, and she couldn't afford another one of those.

Two

→≫≪←

Bailey Tucker had certainly grown up nicely. Ryder started his car and pulled out of the drive. Even covered in river mud, her pretty blue eyes had sparkled in the moonlight, and her wet clothes had clung to some very nice, adult curves. He couldn't remember the last time he'd seen her, but it was probably at least ten or twelve years. She'd been a teenager then, with skinny legs, a long blonde ponytail, blue eyes almost too big for her face, and a smart mouth.

She still had the smart mouth...

Only that mouth now included a pair of full, kissable lips...

He shook that thought out of his head. Being attracted to a woman with the last name of Tucker was asking for trouble. And she'd already made it clear she was on her grandfather's side when it came to the old feud. Her reaction to his proposition had also given him second thoughts about his strategy for approaching her grandfather. He clearly needed a good reason to make Max Tucker hear him out.

Without a new runway, his new business plan for the airfield would be over before it got started.

He still couldn't quite believe a sixty-five-year-old argument between two stubborn men was still going as strong as it was. He thought it was past time for it to be over, but apparently not everyone felt the same way he did. Even Bailey had practically spit out his last name when she'd first recognized him. It had surprised him, because he'd made his peace with her brothers back in high school. But apparently, he needed to make peace with the rest of her family.

He'd have to find the right angle to work.

As he crossed the bridge over the Snake River that separated Eagle's Ridge into two parts—east and west—often thought of as the *haves* and the *havenots* or the *rich side* and the *poor side*—he was reminded of what a huge impact the fight between his grandfather and Bailey's grandfather had had on everyone who had settled in Eagle's Ridge.

His grandfather, John Westbrook, and Bailey's grandfather, Max Tucker, along with two other friends, David Bennett and Will Coleman, had served in the Army Air Corps together in WWII. After the war, they'd made their way to the southeastern part of Washington State, looking for a place to settle. They'd climbed the Blue Mountains and stood on the large ridge overlooking the Snake River and thousands of acres of beautiful land and decided this would be their new home.

All had gone well in the beginning—at least according to his grandfather. John Westbrook was the wealthiest of the four men, so he'd financed much of the land purchase, while each of the other men had bought into their share over time. While his grandfather had taken some of the prime land for himself, he'd said that he'd made sure everyone had some portion of land that was viable for building, farming, whatever...

John and Max, both pilots in the war, along with David, a former flight mechanic, had set up an airfield to bring in supplies and provide an air-taxi service between Eagle's Ridge and other cities. John's sister Margaret and her real-estate developer husband, Ben Garrison, began to build out a town with a general store, a post office, and a school. Will Coleman, who had served as a doctor in the war, set up the first clinic in town that was now a full-service hospital.

But several years into their new lives, John and Max had had a falling out—a drunken poker game and a bad bet, the details of which were not clear—and Max Tucker had ended up losing a big chunk of prime land to John Westbrook, leaving the Tuckers with land on the hillier side of the river. The two men had not spoken since, their feud running through the next generation into his. But Ryder was over it.

The men were both in their nineties now, and Eagle's Ridge had a population of ten-thousand people and an economy that would continue to grow if he could move ahead with his plans to expand the airfield. He'd tried to enlist the help of David Bennett, who had run the airfield since it was built and was still good friends with both Max and John, but David wanted to stay out of it. Will Coleman had made the same claim, saying he'd decided a long time ago not to take sides.

He hadn't spoken to his grandfather yet about his idea. John Westbrook wasn't an easy man to talk to. He was stern, gruff, opinionated, and very judgmental—basically like all the Westbrooks. But it had to be done. And it was past time to do it.

He changed directions at the next intersection. Instead of heading home, he made his way to his grandfather's house. His parents had moved in with his grandfather eight years ago, when it was clear that he needed more help in the house than just a housekeeper, and the two-story, six-bedroom, seven-bathroom house with pool and gardens was plenty big for the three of them. Although, his mother didn't always think so. She'd made a few comments about having to move out of her house and into his grandfather's place, but one day, probably not too far in the distant future, his grandfather would be gone.

It was difficult to imagine such an imposing presence leaving the earth. John Westbrook was turning ninety-five next Tuesday, and while he didn't move as fast as he once did, he was still as mentally sharp as ever, and his blunt words could cut as deep as any knife. Not that John tried to hurt people; he just liked to tell the truth—at least whatever he considered to be the truth—whether they wanted to hear it or not.

As Ryder pulled into the horseshoe-shaped drive in front of the grand home, he couldn't help thinking how ostentatious it was. But that was the Westbrook way. They had the money to have the best, so they had the best. For all intents and purposes, they were considered the first family of Eagle's Ridge: loved by some, hated by others, but rarely thought of with indifference.

He'd forgotten what it meant to have his last name define him. Growing up in Eagle's Ridge with so many expectations, he'd been happy to leave it all behind when he joined the Navy.

But now he was back, and he was going to have to find a way to be himself and also a Westbrook.

He parked his Jeep and went up to the front door to ring the bell. No one had given him a key, and he doubted that was an act of omission. They'd never been the kind of family to have an open door.

A Filipino woman named Leticia greeted him with a smile. In her late sixties now, Leticia had been working for his grandfather for about forty years. She'd moved into the house as a full-time housekeeper about twelve years ago after she and her husband had divorced and her daughter had gone off to college.

She gave him a happy smile and a hug. "Ryder, how lovely to see you."

"You too," he said, stepping into the house. "Is anyone home?"

"Your grandfather is in the den watching his war movies. Your mother is out to dinner with friends, and your father is away for the weekend."

He wasn't surprised to hear that. His father seemed to spend a lot of time away from Eagle's Ridge these days.

"Can I get you something to drink?" she asked.

"A beer would be great."

"I'll bring it into the den."

"Thanks." He walked across the foyer and down the hall, entering the wood-paneled den with its large, brown leather couches, stone fireplace, and massive television screen.

His grandfather, John Westbrook, sat in the middle of the couch, wearing black slacks and a dark-green sweater, his reading glasses sliding down his nose as he glanced up from the book he was reading while watching one of his favorite World War II movies, *The Bridge on the River Kwai.*

"Grandfather," he said, taking a seat in the adjacent armchair. "How are you?"

"Fine." John gave him a suspicious look. "What are you doing here, Ryder? Your mother is out with her girlfriends, and your father is in Seattle."

"I heard. I thought I'd spend some time with you. We haven't had a chance to talk since I got back."

"You've been busy at the airfield. David says you want to expand the runway with Tucker land." His lips curled with distaste. "That won't happen."

He probably should have figured that David would tell his grandfather his plans. He hadn't only forgotten what it meant to be a Westbrook; he'd also forgotten how quickly news traveled. "A longer runway would bring in bigger planes, more tourism, and would benefit everyone in town."

"You think Max Tucker cares about what's good for this town? He only cares about himself."

"His son and his grandsons own businesses here."

"That doesn't matter. Tucker will never sell you his land. He's as stubborn as the day is long. If you'd asked me, I would have told you that, not that you shouldn't have known it already," John said pointedly.

He thought his grandfather could probably give Max Tucker a run for his money in the stubborn department.

"I can't believe David didn't tell you not to bark up that old tree," John continued. "But then David doesn't like to pick sides. He's neutral. He's Switzerland." John shook his head in disgust. "Not picking a side is the coward's way out."

"Aren't you tired of being so angry at someone who was once one of your best friends?" he asked.

His grandfather's eyes widened. "My best friend? I can barely remember when that was true. What I do recall is that Max Tucker betrayed me."

He knew he was about to poke the bear, but he couldn't stop himself. "How exactly did Max do that? I thought you won some of his land in a poker game, and that he was drunk at the time."

"He wasn't that drunk, and that's not when he betrayed me. It was before that. He tried to steal my girl."

"Grandmother?" he asked in surprise.

"Yes. He made a play for Veronica right under my nose. She turned him down, and then he got ass-backward drunk and bet me his land. He said he couldn't lose. Well, he did lose—the game and the girl."

"I never heard that before."

"There's a lot you don't know. It was never just about the land."

He was starting to realize that. "Okay, so, you came out on top. You got the better tracts of land that were easier to develop, and you got Grandma. It seems like you won. Why keep this feud going?"

"He's the one who keeps it going. He's always badmouthing me around town. He takes every opportunity he can to turn people against me. And there have been other incidents over the years. Your father and Tucker's kid, Sam, had some run-ins, too."

"Like what?"

"Ask your dad. He'll tell you."

"Why don't you tell me?"

"Because it upsets me to discuss it."

He didn't think his grandfather looked upset at all. In fact, there was energy in his eyes; maybe it was anger, but it was something.

"You only care about this feud now because you want something," John continued.

His grandfather had a point. "That's true. But what I want will be good for the entire town, not just our side of the river. It's time for us all to come together. I want to end the feud. I want us to have one Founders' Day weekend for all the founders, instead of one day for you and then the next day for everyone else. It's ridiculous."

Now there was no doubting the flames of fury in his grandfather's eyes. "It's not ridiculous. It's about honor, pride, our family name. And it's tradition. People are used to it. I was the first mayor of Eagle's Ridge."

"Being used to something doesn't make it right."

John's gaze narrowed. "What are you asking me to do, Ryder?"

"I don't know—extend an olive branch," he said tentatively. "Or let me do it. Let me tell Max Tucker that you want to end the decades of anger."

John immediately shook his head, disbelief at the suggestion. "That will never happen. I've never done anything wrong. And I will not apologize to that man. Never. Do you hear me, or do I need to say it again?"

His grandfather was practically shouting, and his face was turning dark red.

"What's going on in here?" Leticia asked worriedly, entering the room with his beer.

"Nothing. Ryder is leaving," his grandfather said. "He can take that beer to go."

"I'm sorry I upset you." He got to his feet. "And I won't need that beer after all, Leticia."

"All right." She didn't look happy about his

answer, but she made a quick exit.

He turned his gaze back to his grandfather. "I'll see you another time."

"If you want to expand the runway, build a second one somewhere else, somewhere that doesn't touch Tucker land," his grandfather said. "You don't need the Tuckers to be successful. The Westbrooks make their own way."

He could have pointed out that he'd already looked at all other options, but his grandfather wasn't in the mood for a longer discussion and he didn't want to do anything to cause him physical distress. "I'll think about it." He walked to the door, then paused, glancing over his shoulder

His grandfather had already picked up his book, having probably already forgotten their discussion.

He felt an odd wistfulness that seemed to accompany most conversations he had with his family. He kept wanting there to be something more between them, some feeling of happiness or satisfaction after a good talk, but he always felt...empty.

And it wasn't just with his grandfather that that happened; it was with his mother and father, too. They might look like the beautiful family who had everything on the outside, but inside there was a lot of nothing.

He'd come home, because there was a part of him that wanted to find a way to bring them together. At the moment, he seemed to be driving them further apart.

Three

—➤➤◄◄◄—

Stepping into the No Man's Land diner just after nine on Thursday morning felt like another homecoming. Bailey looked around the restaurant that had been started by her father thirty years ago, and where just about every Tucker had worked at one time or another. This diner was actually a spin-off of the restaurant her grandfather had first started on their side of the river in the early fifties.

When her father, Sam Tucker, had taken control, he had moved the business to the bridge and given it a new name, wanting to put the diner in a neutral location, a place that would welcome customers from both sides of the river.

All residents of Eagle's Ridge were welcome in the rustic restaurant, which boasted a mix of wood-paneled walls and exposed brick, with scarred flooring and windows that overlooked the river. There were still watercolors and oil paintings on display from local artists as well as a sign on one wall that still said *No Fighting*…as if the residents needed a reminder that No Man's Land was a fight-free, feud-free zone.

This morning, the booths that ran around one wall were full, as well as most of the wooden tables in the center of the room and the ten seats at the counter. Breakfast was always one of their most popular meals.

A young, teenaged waitress was taking orders at one table, while a teenaged-male filled coffee cups at another. Behind the counter was Brenda Morgan, a middle-aged, attractive brunette with soft green eyes. Brenda managed the front of the house while Sam Tucker ran the kitchen with the help of two other part-time cooks.

Brenda had been one of her mother's best friends. After her mom had left town to fulfill her own dreams, Brenda had stepped in as a second mom to Bailey, and right now, seeing Brenda's warm green eyes, she almost felt like crying.

She hadn't shed one tear since her life fell apart; she was holding them in, because she had the terrible feeling that once she started crying, she'd never stop.

"Bailey!" Brenda came around the counter with open arms.

She practically ran into Brenda's embrace, hugging her tight.

"Goodness, it is great to see you," Brenda said, as they broke apart. "Your dad said you came home yesterday, but he didn't say why."

Her father, Sam Tucker, came through the kitchen door in time to say, "She didn't tell me why."

"Did you even ask?" Brenda inquired.

Her father gave her a knowing smile. "Bailey always talks in her own time. There's no getting it out of her until she's ready." He paused. "How about some chocolate chip pancakes with whipped cream? Those always used to make you smile."

"When I was seven," she replied.

He groaned. "So, now I suppose you want an egg-white omelet filled with spinach with fruit on the side."

"That sounds perfect. But I also want the chocolate chip pancakes with a big spoonful of whipped cream, too."

"Good, because I've got a batch waiting for you. Coming right up."

As her dad went into the kitchen, she slid into a seat at the counter closest to the cash register.

Brenda poured her a cup of coffee and set it in front of her. "You want some sugar for this, too?"

"I'll save my sugar for the pancakes." She sipped the coffee with genuine appreciation. "Tastes as good as ever. How are you, Brenda?"

"I'm good. Busy as always. What about you?" Brenda's sharp gaze swept her face. "You look tired and stressed. Something is wrong. I told your father that. I said there's no way Bailey just came home for a visit, not in the middle of opening a new restaurant with that handsome celebrity chef."

She licked her lips, not sure how much of her bad news had spread all the way to Eagle's Ridge. "I'm all right. I missed home. I needed a break." She paused, knowing Brenda wouldn't be satisfied with that vague of an answer. "The restaurant didn't work out, and neither did the relationship."

"Oh, honey, I'm sorry."

She sipped her coffee. "I can't talk about it right now."

"I understand. I'm glad you came home. It's the best place to be when you're hurting."

She cleared her throat, not wanting to think about

all the hurt. "What's new around here?"

"Not much. Your father isn't big on change."

"You don't have to tell me that."

Brenda smiled. "No, I don't. Your brothers are working hard on their business, and with all the rain we've been having this winter, the river is still rising every day."

"That should make for some good river trips in the spring and summer," she said, happy that the adventure watersports business her brothers Adam and Zane were running would probably see a boom in business in the next few months. "It's nice to have them out of danger."

"I'll say," Brenda agreed. "Your dad never likes to show his emotions, but he worried a lot with the three of you gone—your brothers in danger zones, you halfway across the world."

"He didn't have to worry about me. I wasn't jumping into raging waters like Adam did while working for the Coast Guard or dodging enemy fire like Zane did with the Army."

"No, but you're his baby, and you were a long way from home. It's nice to have all three of you back home again."

"I'm not going to be here forever. This is just a visit."

"I know. Your dreams have always been bigger than Eagle's Ridge, but it's still good to see your pretty face. Now, I better get back to work."

As Brenda stepped away to help a customer, the door to the diner opened, and Bailey's heart leapt against her chest as Ryder Westbrook walked in. In the shadowy darkness of the night before, she hadn't gotten the perfect look at him, and she'd spent most of the night telling herself he was not that attractive. But she was wrong. He was definitely *that* attractive, and more.

Dressed in dark jeans and a long-sleeved, dark-blue T-shirt that clung to his broad, muscular chest, her mouth went dry. Little shivers ran down her spine when his dark blue gaze settled on her, and a gleam entered his eyes.

There had been a time in her life when she would have died to have Ryder Westbrook look at her like that. As much as she hated his last name, he'd always been one of the most attractive guys in town.

But that was not this time.

She turned back to her coffee cup, hoping he wouldn't come over, but that was a futile thought.

A moment later, he settled into the seat next to hers.

"Morning, Bailey."

"Morning," she murmured, trying not to look at him and hoping her food would appear very soon so she would have something else to focus on.

"Have you thought any more about what we discussed?" he asked.

His words finally forced her gaze to his. "No. I told you there's nothing to be done. My grandfather will never be convinced to sell his land to you. You should let it go."

"I can't let it go. When I want something, I keep after it until I get it."

She couldn't help wondering what it would feel like to be the object of that kind of intense desire. But Ryder wasn't talking about her; he was talking about land—Tucker land.

She broke the connection between them and took

another sip of her coffee, then said, "It's your time to waste."

"It is. I did speak to my grandfather yesterday. He was no more excited about my idea than you were."

"Big surprise."

"He said the feud isn't just about land. That he and your grandfather fought over my grandmother, Veronica."

"Yes. John stole Veronica from my grandpa, and then he took his land. That's what made the betrayal so personal."

"Your grandfather lost the land in a poker game, because he was drunk and he made a bad bet."

"Well, he was drunk, because your grandfather stole the woman he loved. And then he took advantage of his sad state to swindle him out of his land." She could hear her grandfather's voice in her head as she said the same words he'd said so many times.

Ryder, however, didn't look convinced by her argument.

"Obviously, there are two sides," he said. "But I'm guessing that after sixty something years, the story has changed a bit. I doubt anyone really remembers exactly what went down."

She wasn't so sure about that. "Grandpa's short-term memory may waver, but he can tell you exactly what happened sixty-five years ago. He hasn't forgotten a thing."

Ryder let out a sigh. "Your grandfather got married. He had a kid, grandkids, and has lived a good, long life. Don't you think he could find it in his heart to look at what happened a bit differently?"

"You just told me your grandfather couldn't. Why

should mine be any different?"

"Good point," he conceded.

"And it's not just John Westbrook my grandfather can't forgive; it's himself. He has always felt guilty for losing land that could have provided more wealth and better opportunities for the family. It's a deep pain inside of him. He's as harsh a judge of himself as he is of others."

"I get it, Bailey, but you see that a bigger airport could benefit this town, don't you? We need tourism dollars—for this diner, for your brothers' business, for everyone here—on both sides of the river."

"I don't disagree. I just don't think you'll be able to use Tucker land. But if you want to talk to my grandfather, go for it."

"I will talk to him, but you've made me realize I need a better strategy. Maybe you could talk to him before I do, feel him out."

"I really don't want to get involved. I have a lot of my own problems right now."

"At least tell me more about him—help me come up with a plan, give me some tips."

"I don't know how long I'm going to be around."

"Probably until the publicity dies down, right?" he said.

She let out a small gasp, her eyes widening as she realized he knew what had happened in New York. "What do you know?"

"What I read on the internet. I'd love to hear it from you."

She saw her father heading out of the kitchen with her breakfast. "Please don't say anything about it here."

"Ryder," her father said with a welcoming smile.

"I was wondering when you'd make your way in here. I heard you were in town. It's good to see you again."

"Thanks. You, too, Mr. Tucker."

"Oh, please, it's Sam."

Her dad set her omelet and side of chocolate chip pancakes down in front of her, making her feel a little embarrassed by how much she had ordered.

"What can I get you?" her dad asked Ryder.

"What Bailey is having looks good," he replied.

"The healthy eggs or the sugary pancakes that were always her favorite?"

"Both."

"Coming right up."

"So, you haven't been in here since you got back?" Bailey asked, as her father returned to the kitchen. "Quite a coincidence that you came in today."

"Not a coincidence at all; I was looking for you."

Her heart made another unstoppable leap. She knew Ryder's interest in her was only because of her connection to her grandfather, so she needed to stop letting old schoolgirl fantasies run through her head.

"Why don't you just get Adam or Zane to help you? They live here. They'll benefit from the runway. They can add a personal perspective if they speak to my grandfather."

"Do you really want me to talk to Zane again? I might slip up and mention something about rescuing his dog from the river."

She saw the sly gleam in his eyes. "You cannot do that. Zane doesn't need to know anything about last night."

"I might be more able to forget about it if you were willing to help me."

"You're blackmailing me?"

"Let's just say I'm trying to get us what we both want."

She realized that her desire to keep Gambler's outing from her brother had given Ryder some leverage. "Typical Westbrook maneuver," she said dryly.

"Ouch," he said with a smile. "But I can't deny that I didn't learn a little something from my grandfather."

"Fine. What's it going to take to keep you quiet? A conversation with my grandfather?"

"Not yet. Like I said, I want to make a plan. I'm going to get one shot at Max Tucker, and I want to make it count."

"Then what?"

"Dinner—tonight. You're buying."

"And you're pushing it, Ryder."

"What time do you want me to pick you up?"

She suddenly realized that she didn't want to go out to dinner with Ryder anywhere in the small town of Eagle's Ridge, where gossip was a professional sport. She thought for a moment. "Where do you live? Are you staying at your parents' house?"

"No. I have a house on Riverview."

"And you live alone? No wife or girlfriend?"

"I'm on my own," he said. "Why?"

"I'll bring you dinner, or I'll cook," she said impulsively, even though cooking was almost as high on her list of things she didn't want to do as having dinner with Ryder. She hadn't chopped an onion or turned on a burner since the debacle at Franco's restaurant a week ago.

"That works for me," Ryder said.

"I'll meet you there. What's the address?"

"Eleven twenty-seven."

"Great. I'll be there at seven." She turned her attention back to her breakfast, digging into her eggs with a sigh of delight.

"Good, huh?" Ryder asked with amusement.

"My dad has always been the master of breakfast. You'll see," she added, as Brenda set two plates in front of Ryder.

"I'm good at lunch and dinner, too," her dad said, popping his head back through the pass-through window with a smile. "Maybe not as good as you are, Princess, but not bad."

"You taught me everything I know."

Her dad smiled. "Only the basics. You did the rest."

As her father disappeared into the kitchen, she watched Ryder take his first bite and then groan with satisfaction.

"Really good," he said.

"Told you." She moved on to her pancakes.

"If you're half as good a cook as your father, I can't wait for dinner."

His words reminded her of the bargain she'd just made—one she was already regretting. Before she had time to answer, she heard two familiar voices behind her.

Turning her head, she saw her twin brothers Adam and Zane walk through the door. They were greeted by locals at various tables, and as always, their presence made an impact.

Fraternal twins, Adam and Zane, had very similar features with light-blue, almost turquoise eyes, a family eye color passed down from her mother's side of the family.

Her brothers were both tall, powerful, ruggedly attractive men. Sometimes, she couldn't quite believe that Zane, who had been sickly for most of his childhood, had actually passed Adam by an inch, ringing in somewhere around six four. Not that Adam would admit that his twin had surpassed him in any way. She'd never met two more competitive men. But despite their sibling rivalry, they were close; they even shared a business now, and things seemed to be going well.

As Ryder stood up to greet Adam and Zane, she was a little surprised by the warm friendliness extended by her brothers. Was she the only one hanging on to the Westbrook-Tucker feud besides her grandfather?

"Let's all get a table," Zane suggested. "We can catch up."

"I'm actually done," she put in. "You guys go ahead." She decided to skip the rest of her pancakes in favor of a quick exit.

As she slid off her seat, Adam said, "We need to talk, Bailey. What happened in New York? I thought you were in the middle of a big restaurant opening, that your career was so important that it took every minute of your time, including the holidays."

She heard the censure in his tone and knew that no one had been happy about her missing Thanksgiving and Christmas the previous year. She was just relieved that he didn't seem to know what had happened in New York. She would have to tell both of them, but she had no intention of sharing the sordid details in the middle of the diner.

"I was busy," she said. "But that's done, and I needed a break, so here I am. And let's not forget how many holidays the two of you missed while you were in the Coast Guard and the Army. Anyway, we'll talk later. I have some things to do."

"What things?" Zane asked curiously.

"Yeah, why are you being so mysterious?" Adam pressed. "We thought you might want to come by and help us get the kayaks ready for the upcoming season."

"I'll come by later. We'll talk then."

She could see the questions lingering in her brothers' eyes but she wasn't ready to answer any of them. Maybe coming home hadn't been the greatest idea after all. She knew that her brothers would be supportive, but she wasn't ready to bare her soul and share her stupidity just yet. As the youngest in the family, and the only girl, her brothers had always been protective of her, and they'd always had opinions about her life. She wasn't ready to hear any of those opinions now.

She glanced back at Brenda. "Tell Dad I'll catch up with him this afternoon."

"Will do," Brenda said with a smile. "Have fun, Bailey."

"Thanks."

"Hey, Bailey," Zane said, making her pause once more. "Thanks again for watching Gambler last night. Did he give you any trouble?"

"Not a bit," she said, seeing the smile play across Ryder's lips.

He'd keep her secret. He wanted something from her, and she wanted something from him. They'd have dinner. She'd listened to his plan to end the family feud, and then they'd say goodbye and that would be that.

Four

─➤➤❮❮◄─

After leaving the diner, Bailey walked across Sentinel Bridge, heading into town. She hadn't been home in over a year, because she'd been too busy working as a chef and helping Franco open his new restaurant. She'd told herself that it was worth it. She was doing what she loved, but now, after everything that had happened, she couldn't help wondering if the choices she'd made had been even a little bit smart. Frowning, she decided to push New York out of her mind for a while and get reacquainted with her hometown.

She paused by the two statues at the end of the bridge, their likenesses representing founders John Westbrook and Will Coleman. Two other statues on the opposite end of the bridge represented Max Tucker and David Bennett. The four men had been looking for a place to start over, to put down roots after the war, and a hiking trip in the Blue Mountains had presented an incredible vista of opportunity.

While she'd told Ryder what her grandfather had always told her, she didn't really know all the ins and outs of the feud. It had happened decades before she was born, and the retelling always seemed to take on a new twist or turn. It was quite possible her grandfather didn't remember everything exactly the way it had happened. It was also quite possible that Ryder's grandfather John Westbrook didn't, either. But that wasn't going to be enough to change either of their stubborn minds.

Her phone buzzed and she sighed as she saw another flood of texts from concerned friends and also the press. She was on the other side of the country, but it still wasn't far enough. She could throw her phone into the river. On the other hand, she wasn't quite ready to cut all ties to New York, so she put the phone back into her pocket and kept on walking.

She headed through the park and then into downtown, noting several new clothing boutiques, an art gallery, a bookstore, and a pizza place that must have opened in the last year. But along with the new was also the old: Hildie's House—a place for antiques—or junk as the locals called it; the grand Broadleaf hotel; the majestic courthouse; and, of course, the donut shop, which had been very popular both before and after school.

There were plenty of people around on a Thursday morning, and she tried to stay in the shadows, veering away from familiar faces when she saw them coming her way. While Eagle's Ridge was on the other side of the country from New York, the internet had a way of making the world very small.

Her phone rang again, a call this time, not a text. She pulled it out of her pocket to check the number.

Her heart went into her throat—*Franco.*

She couldn't believe he was calling her now.

What on earth could he possibly have to say? She wanted to know, and she didn't want to know.

She let the call go to voicemail and hoped he wouldn't leave a message, because she really didn't want to hear his voice, his explanations or his apologies. Not that she should assume he would apologize; he certainly hadn't so far.

She needed to put her mind onto something else, and as she saw the market up ahead, she knew just what she needed to think about—dinner. She'd told Ryder she'd bring him dinner, but maybe she would make something at his house, so she wouldn't have to stop anywhere to pick up food.

Entering the market, she grabbed a cart and felt immediately happier when she walked into the produce section. There were two supermarkets in Eagle's Ridge: a chain grocer that carried the more affordable basics, and this one—a gourmet market filled with organic produce and expensive cuts of meat. She was actually impressed with how the market had upped its game in the last several years.

The prices had gone up, too, but they didn't put her off. The produce looked incredibly fresh, and already her brain was spinning with ideas of what she could make. Cooking had always been her therapy, her escape when life got too hard—when her mother had left, when her brothers were in the service and in danger, and when she'd left her small, safe hometown to venture into the world.

But now it felt like forever since she'd really cooked for pleasure. The past few years had all been about technique, skills, impressing people, and most recently executing other chefs' visions, not her own.

She picked up a dark-green avocado, happy with

the slightly softened feel. It was perfect. She grabbed two more and then moved down to the green beans, the asparagus and the peppers. While she loved meat and fish, making vegetables taste good was also a passion of hers.

"Bailey Tucker?"

She tensed, not quite able to place the voice, but when she looked up to see one of her former high school teachers—Diana Woods—she blew out a breath of relief. Former teachers she could handle. Friends with lots of questions were a different story.

Tall and voluptuous with thick, dark-red hair and green eyes, Miss Woods was about forty and as attractive as ever. When Bailey had been in high school, Miss Woods had been very popular with the high school boys. But looks aside, her caring personality had also made her popular with the girls, who'd found a mentor and a friend in a woman only about ten years older than they were.

"Miss Woods," she said, genuinely happy to see her. "I can't believe you remember me after all this time."

"Well, I did spend more time with your brothers when I had to oversee detention," Miss Woods said dryly. "But I still remember you and the amazing meal you made for the teacher's lunch your senior year. As soon as I tasted your paella, I understood why I could never get you interested in history. You were destined to be a chef. I had never eaten anything so good. In fact, I've tried to replicate it a few times but I've always been unsuccessful. I wonder if you could give me the recipe sometime."

"I don't remember that exact recipe—I probably made it up. But I could come up with something."

"Really? That would be so nice of you. I promised someone I'd make him dinner one night, and I'd like it to be good," she said with a sheepish smile.

Bailey couldn't help wondering who that *someone* was, but she couldn't bring herself to ask.

"Are you visiting your family?" Miss Woods asked.

"Yes, for a short time. I haven't been home in a while."

"I'm sure they're thrilled to have you back. Your father is always bragging about you when I stop in at the diner. He likes to say you got your cooking skills from him, by the way."

"I'm sure I did. He was my first teacher. Mom was an okay cook, but Dad was a wizard in the kitchen, especially with breakfast. No one did chocolate chip pancakes better than him, and he's still going strong. I just had some of his pancakes at the diner."

"I've had his pancakes, too, not with chocolate chips, but that sounds decadent."

"Oh, it is, trust me."

"And you're a chef in New York City, right?"

She nodded, her tension coming back.

"I'm so glad you were able to do exactly what you were meant to do," Miss Woods said. "Dreams can come true."

"Being a chef was really all I ever wanted to be," she murmured, unexpected moisture coming into her eyes. Her emotions were awfully close to the surface these days and being reminded of her long-ago youthful dreams and how she'd pretty much destroyed everything by trusting the wrong person made her feel more than a little choked up. "I have to go. It was nice to see you."

"You, too."

She quickly wheeled her cart out of the produce section and headed to the meat and seafood department, wanting to finish her shopping and get out of the market as soon as possible. As she waited for her order to be filled, she couldn't help thinking about what Miss Woods had said—that she'd been destined to be a chef.

Maybe getting back into a kitchen would be the first step in figuring out how to fix her life.

———»»«««———

Ryder took a quick look around his living room, making sure he hadn't missed any errant socks or empty glasses. Over a decade in the military had instilled a sense of neatness into him, but since he'd left the Navy last month and bought the two-bedroom house by the river, he'd gotten a little lax when it came to cleaning up his space the instant he was done with it.

The room was in good enough shape—a little sparse when it came to decorating—but the oversized cream-colored couch with the soft cushions and the brown leather recliner that faced a stone fireplace and a large television were perfect for his needs. Eventually, he had plans to remodel the kitchen and the bedrooms, maybe build a second story, but that was way down the road.

The only construction he was interested in now had to do with the airport. If he couldn't expand the runway, he'd never be able to do everything he wanted to do, and that wasn't an option. He wanted to live in

Eagle's Ridge. He wanted to spend the next chapter of his life here. Sometimes he couldn't even quite believe that, but it was true.

Hopefully, after talking to Bailey, he could come up with a better plan of attack to get her grandfather on his side.

Thinking about Bailey brought a smile to his face. She'd been so unsettled at the diner earlier, especially when Adam and Zane had come in. She'd probably worried he was going to tell Zane about Gambler's misadventure, but that thought had never entered his mind. He had a small bit of leverage over her, and he was going to use it.

He didn't really know why she cared what Zane thought. It wasn't like her brothers hadn't gotten into all kinds of trouble back in the day, but he did know that the Tuckers were very competitive. Adam and Zane were always betting on whether one could outdo the other. He'd even got sucked into one of those bets back in high school, which had landed him in detention for several weeks during the spring semester of his senior year. It was the first and only time in his life he'd ever been in detention.

It had been a blessing in disguise, though. That was when he'd gotten to know Adam and Zane, and a bunch of other kids who came from the *other* side of the river, when he'd realized that Tuckers were real people, not just his grandfather's mortal enemies.

But obviously Bailey still saw him as an evil Westbrook. She hadn't even wanted to take his hand when she'd gotten stuck in the mud. Only a desire to get out of the watery marsh had made her accept his help, and he doubted she was even half as stubborn as her grandfather. He probably had his work cut out with both of them.

He walked over to the window and glanced outside, seeing nothing much beyond his empty driveway and the dark skulking trees that lined his property. It was a little past seven, and the sun had set a half hour ago. There was only a sliver of a moon tonight, and it disappeared in and out of the clouds as rain was forecasted for later in the night.

Hopefully, Bailey would actually show up. Ending-the-feud plans aside, he was looking forward to seeing her again. In fact, his stomach had been twisting itself into unexpected knots for the past few hours.

He hadn't felt that gut-clenching, heart-stopping, burst of attraction in a long time. And it wasn't just that Bailey was a beautiful blonde with blue eyes that reminded him of the sky he spent so much time in; it was also her personality, her fire, her stubborn independence. The fact that she didn't like him at all had only made her more interesting. He liked a challenge, and he was determined to make sure that if she was going to dislike him, she was going to have to find a good reason other than his last name.

Car lights flashed as she pulled into his driveway. He drew in a rough breath of anticipation, feeling oddly nervous, and that wasn't like him. He'd flown across enemy lines, crashed behind one of those lines, had more than one near-death experience, so he really shouldn't have sweaty palms because of one hot blonde.

Focus, he ordered himself, as he headed toward the door. This wasn't a date, and he had a lot riding on this dinner; he couldn't let himself forget that.

He met her at her car, as she pulled two grocery

bags out of the backseat. He was happy to see that she was planning on cooking and that she hadn't brought him a ready-made meal. That would give them more time to get better acquainted.

"Let me help," he said, taking both bags as she reached back into the car for her purse. "Looks like you're cooking."

"It looks that way," she muttered, not sounding too happy about it.

Well, she was here; that was all that mattered.

"This is nice," she murmured, as they walked through the front door and into the living room. "Very masculine."

"Well, I'm the only one here. It needs more stuff, but I haven't had time."

"Did you buy this place or are you renting?"

"I bought the house and moved in two weeks ago."

She nodded. "Of course you did—you're a Westbrook. I doubt anyone in your family has ever been a renter."

"That might be true. The Westbrooks have made most of their money in real-estate and construction. But aside from that, I've been living on military bases for most of the last decade, so it felt like the right time to have a more permanent address. There was a part of me that needed to make a commitment to starting something new, so I made the deal." He abruptly stopped talking, wondering why he'd told her that.

She gave him a thoughtful look but didn't comment. "The kitchen?"

"Right this way." He led her across the hall, relieved she hadn't asked him any more personal questions about his decision to come home. "I should have probably warned you that the kitchen is not completely decked out," he added. "I have basic pots and pans, plates and silverware, but not a lot of fancy gadgets. I've been living off cans of soup, barbecued chicken and take-out."

"I don't need fancy. I've always been able to make do; I didn't grow up rich."

He set the bags down on the table and gave her a smile. "You didn't exactly grow up poor, either."

"How would you know?"

"The diner does a good business."

She shrugged. "There's money and then there's Westbrook money."

"Probably true," he conceded. "I cannot apologize for my family's ability to make a lot of money. They're very good at it. And, by the way, you can insult me all you want, but you owe me dinner, and you're making good on it."

"Obviously, that's why I'm here. I'm not trying to get out of dinner. Tuckers always keep their end of a deal."

"Ah, another thinly veiled insult. You got anything else, or should we start unpacking?"

She sighed, apology in her eyes. "I'm sorry, Ryder. You're right. I'm being rude."

He was startled by her words, not completely sure he could trust them. "Okay."

"It's been a long week, and I am way off my game. I'm not even sure I can cook you a good meal. I haven't been in a kitchen since…" Her voice faded away, as her gaze moved around the room.

"Since you allegedly cooked a dish that sent twenty people to the hospital with food poisoning and destroyed the reputation of a top chef and a new restaurant?" he queried.

Her lips tightened. "Well, I'm glad you said *allegedly*; I don't think the article you read actually said that."

"Is it true?"

"Are you worried I'm going to poison you?"

"Judging by how unhappy you are to be here, I probably should be, but I'm not. Want to tell me your side of the story, Bailey?"

"Not really." Her blue eyes filled with shadows. "But if you still want me to cook, I will do my best not to send you to the hospital."

"I would appreciate that. I've already spent too much time in a hospital."

Her gaze sharpened, and he suddenly realized he'd said too much.

"You were hurt?" she asked. "Is that why you left the Navy?"

"It's not *why* I left, but I did suffer some injuries after a hard landing. I broke my arm and cracked a couple of ribs, but I survived," he said, glossing over the incident.

"When was that?"

"Six months ago."

"What happened?"

"The helo I was flying took enemy fire. I had to set her down."

"That sounds terrifying. Where were you?"

"It doesn't matter."

"You can't say?"

"I can't."

"Well, can you tell me if everyone survived?"

"Thankfully, yes."

Relief flashed in her eyes, and he was surprised

that she'd been even a little worried about people she didn't know.

"I'm so glad," she said. "Growing up in Eagle's Ridge, where so many young men and women go off to serve and don't always come back, I always worry every time I see news about someone killed in action."

He could understand that. Eagle's Ridge was a military town, steeped in the tradition of service, and almost all of his friends had gone into some branch of the military after high school.

"I lived in fear of something happening to Zane or Adam when they were serving," Bailey added. "I was so relieved when they both decided to get out. I'm sure your family is happy you're back."

"Probably."

Her gaze narrowed. "You don't know?"

"We don't share personal feelings in my family."

"Well, I'm quite certain they're relieved to have you out of harm's way."

"I suppose so. They never wanted me to join the Navy. Besides my grandfather, Westbrooks tend to buck the tradition of service, although my mother claims that she serves in her own way by running half the fundraisers in town," he said dryly.

"Well, she does raise a lot of money for various charities, so she's right." Bailey paused. "You said you didn't leave the Navy because of the crash or your injuries, so why did you leave? Eagle's Ridge must seem awfully quiet."

"Quiet and good. And my reasons are...complicated."

"Are they? Or do you just not like to share personal feelings, either?"

"I have to admit that's probably the one area

where I do take after my family," he acknowledged. "Shall we get started on dinner? Is there anything I can help you with?" He was eager to get the conversation away from his personal life.

"I don't think you can help me, considering you just told me you've been living off canned soup and barbecue."

"That's true, but I can wash vegetables and chop. It looks like you got a lot of produce."

"There were so many great choices at the store, I couldn't decide what I wanted."

"What are you making?"

"No idea yet," she said with a small smile. "I'm going to let the ingredients speak to me. And I will let you be my prep chef, but on one condition."

"What's that?"

"No talking about feuds and grandfathers until after dinner."

That was fine by him. At the moment, he was more interested in getting to know her. "Deal."

"Why don't you wash and slice the mushrooms?" She pulled a band off her wrist and swept her hair up into a ponytail. "Then you can move on to the peppers."

"Got it."

While he started on the mushrooms, Bailey opened up his cabinets and pulled out pots and pans, placing them on the stove. Then she looked at the array of ingredients on the table. Despite her claim that the vegetables would tell her what to do, she didn't seem to be in a hurry to get started. After a few moments, she folded her arms across her waist and let out a sigh.

"Problem?" he asked. "Vegetables aren't talking

to you? No one is eager to get cooked up in some delicious meal?"

She gave him a distracted look. "What?"

"Okay, that was a little funny," he told her.

"Sorry, I didn't hear what you said."

"What's going on?" he asked, seeing what looked like panic flash through her eyes.

"I haven't been able to cook since…"

"Oh," he said, beginning to realize that whatever had happened in New York had definitely traumatized her.

"It's ridiculous," she said, waving a wild hand in the air. "I'm a chef. It's what I do; what I love to do; what I was born to do. It's been my life, my *whole* life, every waking second for as long as I can remember. Now, I feel suddenly terrified."

She blinked a few times, and he was worried she was about to burst into tears, and he had no idea what he was going to do then.

"You don't have to cook," he said quickly. "We'll go out, or we'll order in. It's not a big deal."

"I can't be a quitter. Tuckers aren't quitters."

"You're not quitting. You're just taking a minute."

"I've already taken almost a week. I hate that he's taken this away from me, too."

Ryder didn't know who *he* was, but he instinctively disliked him. "Then don't let him," he said. "We'll cook together. I've got eggs. You brought lots of vegetables. We'll make an omelet."

She drew in a breath, squared her shoulders, and lifted her chin. "No, you're not going to eat an omelet for dinner. I can do this. I can make you a really good meal."

"I know you can," he said quietly.

She met his gaze. "I didn't poison those people in New York. I didn't cook the meal that they ate no matter what the owner said."

"I believe you."

"Thank you. Not many people do."

"Why not?"

"Because the chef, the owner of the restaurant, is Franco Dubois. He is a renowned three-star Michelin chef from Paris. He owns a dozen restaurants around the world. He's brilliant and acclaimed and he told everyone that I was responsible for the food poisoning and then he fired me."

Anger ran through him at the pain in her eyes. "You can still set the record straight, Bailey. You just have to make people listen."

"Even if I got the press to print retractions, it wouldn't matter. The restaurant world is very incestuous. Everyone knows everybody and what Franco said will always make people doubt me."

"Then you'll find a way to get rid of the doubt."

"You say that like it's easy."

"Not easy, but I think you can do it. When you're ready."

"I'm not ready to take on the press or the food writers or Franco, but I am ready to make you some dinner."

"It's a good place to start."

"Okay then, I just have to make some decisions. Let's see." She took another moment and then said, "I think I will do a spinach salad with mushrooms and bacon, roasted red peppers with goat cheese, and I have a beautiful wild salmon that I can top with a wonderful sauce. How does that sound?"

"Like the best meal I've had in a long time."

"I don't think you've set the bar very high, but I'll take it."

"Then let's get on with it, because now you've made me even more hungry."

Five

Once she started cooking, Bailey's instincts kicked in, and she stopped thinking about how badly everything had gone the past week and focused instead on the meal she was making. It was simple and not at all difficult to make, but her competitive spirit was getting back into gear, and she wanted it to be the best meal that Ryder had had in a very long time.

He was a surprisingly good prep cook, following her instructions with little comment, and for the most part they worked in an unusually comfortable silence considering the fact that they really didn't know each other at all.

Aside from their conversation last night and this morning, she'd probably spoken ten words to him in her entire life. She'd always known of him, of course, because he had been in her brothers' grade, and he was well-known around town, not only because of his last name, but because of all of his athletic and academic accomplishments.

She doubted Ryder knew much about her younger

self, since she had had no athletic or academic accomplishments of note. High school had not been the best time of her life.

She'd thought her twenties were much better, until last week...

But that was last week. She needed to stay in the present and start looking forward.

While she finished plating, Ryder set the small kitchen table and opened the bottle of wine she'd brought to pair with her fish.

"I'm pouring you a glass," he told her.

"Please," she said. "I am more than ready for some wine."

He smiled. "I'm more than ready for that food."

She brought the salmon and the spinach salad to the table while Ryder retrieved a plate of stuffed red peppers and a bowl of jasmine rice that she'd made to go with the fish. As they sat down together, she was rather proud of what she'd whipped up.

"I can't believe you did all this in an hour, and I was even watching you do it," Ryder said. "You're a magician, Bailey."

"It was a bit easier having your help," she admitted, taking a sip of her wine. "You aren't bad with a knife."

"Not a skill I thought I had, but okay," he said with a laugh.

"You're really good at everything, aren't you?"

"I wouldn't say everything."

"Oh, yeah, then tell me something you're not good at, Mr. Student Body President, High School Quarterback, Star Baseball Player, Most Likely to Succeed..."

"Did you look me up in the high school yearbook

before you came over?"

"I didn't have to. I grew up here and in a house with two brothers who both admired and hated you at various times in their lives."

"I hope they didn't actually hate me."

"They probably didn't, since you led a lot of their teams to victory. But maybe a little jealous. Adam and Zane like to win—a lot."

"So do I." He paused, as he scooped some rice onto his plate. "So do you."

"Not in sports, but in the kitchen, yes. Anyway, eat before it gets cold."

"You don't have to tell me twice," he said, as he took a bite of the stuffed pepper. "Amazing. I've never been a fan of bell peppers, but stuffed with goat cheese and whatever else you put in here has changed my mind."

"Anything can be great if you know how to cook it. But you should have told me you don't like peppers."

"Are you kidding? I figured I was on thin ice just getting you over here."

"You were on thin ice. I didn't like being blackmailed."

"I wouldn't have told Zane about Gambler's great escape if you'd said no."

She raised a brow. "Now you tell me that?"

"Come on, you weren't really worried, were you?"

"Obviously, I was, or I wouldn't be here right now." Actually, that wasn't completely true, but she wasn't going to tell him that. She could hardly say she'd let him blackmail her because she'd wanted to get to know him. That would be crazy.

"Maybe you just wanted to see me again, Bailey." He gave her a charming, sexy smile that sent tingles down her spine. Now she had a better understanding of why Ryder had been so popular with the girls in high school. When he smiled, there was no way a woman couldn't smile back. She dragged her gaze away from his and concentrated on her dinner.

She hadn't felt hungry in almost a week, but since she'd returned to Eagle's Ridge, she was definitely making up for her lack of calories in the days preceding.

As she finished her meal, she sat back and picked up her glass of wine, feeling more relaxed than she had in a long time. But as Ryder wiped his sexy mouth with a napkin, a gleam entered his eyes, and she had a feeling her chill mood was going to be on its way out very soon.

"That was excellent, Bailey."

"Thank you."

"I'm glad you found your way back into the kitchen."

"It only took a little blackmail to get me there."

"Consider it my good deed."

"I wouldn't go that far. But I think returning to Eagle's Ridge was probably the best idea I've had in months."

"Sometimes it's good to get back to your roots," he agreed.

"Yes, it is. Earlier today, when I went to the market, I ran into Miss Woods. I don't know if you remember her from high school. She was my history teacher."

"Of course, I remember Miss Woody."

She frowned. "You mean, Miss Woods."

"Uh, yeah, Miss Woody is what the guys called her," he said with a somewhat sheepish expression. "It was a stupid joke."

It took a minute for the nickname to register. "Oh. I get it."

"She was hot and about twenty-six, I think. We were eighteen and pretty stupid. She ran detention, which gave us a lot of time to look at her."

"I never went to detention, but I know my brothers spent a lot of time there. Now, I'm starting to think that's because they wanted to see Miss Woods."

"It wasn't the worst punishment; I'll say that. Not that Miss Woods was ever that friendly to any of us. She treated us like irritating boys."

"Which you all were—at least, my brothers were. I am a little surprised you were there, Ryder. You weren't the kind of kid to be in detention. You were always running things, breaking school records, getting awards of achievement. You weren't just blessed with talent; you had brains, too."

"My cousin Ford Garrison and I got caught up in one of Zane's bets."

"I didn't even know you were friends with Zane."

"We didn't know each other too well before that, but once we were in detention together, we got closer. In fact, there was a group of us that hung together. I think Zane called us the Gang of Seven."

"Who was in the gang?" she asked curiously.

"Your two brothers, me and Ford, Noah Coleman, Jack Carter, and Wyatt Chandler."

She thought about all the guys he'd just mentioned, every single one of whom had gone on to the military. "You were all in there together? I'm a little surprised, because you all went on to join the military. Funny that you went from delinquents to heroes."

"We weren't that bad, just bored with high school, and eager to get on with our lives. I was actually happy that I ended up in detention, because it was the first time I really got to know your brothers and some of the other guys. We all grew up in the same town, went to the same schools, but the damn feud between our families spread across town in so many ways, making enemies of people who didn't even know each other."

"That's true," she admitted.

"But we all grew up with one thing in common— an expectation that we'd serve in some way."

She nodded. "I've often felt guilty that I didn't join one of the military branches. I just never wanted to be a soldier." She paused. "And don't say the expectation was less for me because I'm a woman. I still grew up here. I grieved with families and friends who lost fathers and brothers and sons. I just didn't have it in me."

His gaze met hers, understanding in his eyes. "It's not for everyone. You shouldn't feel guilty. We all contribute to the world in some way and feeding people is important."

"You're being nice," she said, sipping her wine. "Is that because you're still trying to butter me up?"

"I'm not trying to play you, Bailey. I believe what I just said. And frankly, my reasons for going into the Navy were not as altruistic as you might think. I wanted to fly really cool helicopters, and you know where you find those…"

"In the Navy," she said with a smile, liking him even more for his honesty.

"Exactly. Now, let's get back to what you were saying before we got off track. You had a conversation with Miss Woods?"

"Yes. She told me she still remembered the paella that I made for the teachers' thank-you lunch my senior year in high school. After she tasted my food, it was completely clear to her why I had never been interested in history; I was destined to be a chef. It was nice to be reminded of just how far back my passion for cooking goes. In the pursuit of my ambitions, I forgot the joy that cooking brings me, whether it's for one person or a hundred. Anyway, between you and Miss Woods, you got me back in the kitchen again."

"And you made an incredible meal." He cocked his head to the right, giving her a thoughtful look. "What happened in New York, Bailey?"

"It's a long story."

"We've got some time."

"You already looked me up. You know most of it."

"But not all of it."

She didn't know what to think about his curiosity. He'd said he wasn't playing her, but was that completely true? Maybe he just wanted to get to know her so he could figure out how to manipulate her.

Or…was she making him into Franco, the last man who'd wanted to get to know her and then had used her and thrown her away?

"Bailey," he prodded.

"I don't know if I can trust you, Ryder."

"Do you need to trust me? It's only a matter of time before the news gets out. I'm sure I'm not the only one who's curious about your sudden return home. I doubt whatever you tell me will be a secret for long, if it even is now."

She was glad he hadn't tried to persuade her to trust him. Somehow, it made him seem more trustworthy, which didn't really make sense, but it was the way she felt. "Fine. Here's the short version of the story. Last year, I had the opportunity to work as an executive chef for a world- renowned chef and restauranteur, Franco Dubois. It was exciting to be in his kitchen. He's a brilliant, talented, charismatic man, very handsome, very charming."

"You fell in love with him."

"Stupidly, yes. I knew that he'd been married and divorced, that there had been a lot of women in his life, but I thought I was different, that we had a special connection. It wasn't just personal; it was professional, too. When we cooked together, we created amazing dishes, and somehow that carried over into the idea that we could be amazing other places besides the kitchen."

She sipped her wine, then continued. "When Franco offered me the opportunity to open a new French restaurant with him in Tribeca, I was thrilled. I spent months thinking about ingredients, scouring farms, talking to butchers and fishermen, planning the décor, finding the best of everything. The closer we got to opening day, the more strained my relationship with Franco became. We were bickering over menu designs and kitchen tiles and not spending any time together." She paused, thinking back over the last year. "I thought I could have it all, but I ended up with nothing."

"Because something went wrong on opening day. How did the people get sick?"

"We were in a rush. We never should have opened. We weren't ready. We'd had a lot of issues, but one in particular with one of our fish suppliers. I didn't like the fish we'd gotten that day. I told Franco we had to adjust the menu, go all meat and vegetables for opening night, but he said he would find a way to get some good fish, that it was part of his signature dish, which it was. I was too busy to think about what he was doing. In the end, he didn't get any new fish; he simply told the fish supplier who had provided the first bad batch to send some more over. He didn't check it when it came in, and neither did I. It was bad, and people got sick, and Franco told everyone that I knew the fish wasn't up to par and that I served it anyway. He went on to imply that I'd done it on purpose out of personal jealousy because he was seeing someone else, and I couldn't take it."

The last part still stung, but it also made her angry.

"He sucks," Ryder said bluntly.

"He does."

"Was he seeing someone else?"

"Yes. I told you I was stupid."

"Why didn't you tell the truth, Bailey? You're a woman who speaks her mind. Why didn't you fight for your reputation?"

"I tried, but people were more interested in talking about my relationship with Franco and the A-list actress he'd been sleeping with while I was putting his restaurant together. I had thought work was what was coming between us, but it turns out there was a woman, too. Anyway, I just stopped answering my phone. I should have made a stronger statement about what happened. I was just so shocked and hurt and angry—not just at him but at myself."

"I can understand that."

"I wish I could go back and do things differently."

"But you can't. You can only move forward. And for the record, it doesn't sound to me like you did anything wrong in the restaurant that night."

"I probably should have checked the fish again. I was supposed to be watching everything that left the kitchen. I just assumed that because it was his signature dish, one that he actually took pride in making, that he had overseen it with an eye to every detail. But he was busy that night. He kept leaving the kitchen to talk to friends and food writers. I should have spoken up. I should have used my voice, which I'm beginning to realize now got quieter and quieter the longer I worked with him."

She cleared her throat. "Anyway, Franco fired me to save the reputation of the restaurant, all the money he'd invested. He shut down after opening night, announced he had fired the entire staff, and that he would be reopening next month with an entirely new crew. I don't know if that will be enough to convince anyone to come back; I guess we'll see."

"It would serve him right if no one came back. He's to blame for this, Bailey."

"Even if he is, I feel badly for everyone who worked at the restaurant. We were a team, and Franco and I both let them down. At any rate, that's a longer version than I meant to tell you. It must be the wine; I'm way too talkative tonight."

"Perhaps you needed to get it out."

"Maybe. You're the first person I've told around here. Not even my family knows, although I'm going to have to tell them."

"They'll have your back."

"I know. I just wish they didn't have to. I hate making mistakes, Ryder. I hate it so much. I like to win."

He gave her a smile of complete understanding. "I feel exactly the same way. You'll win again, Bailey; tonight was a start. You'll get back in a bigger kitchen; I'm sure of it. You are a stubborn Tucker after all."

"I hope so." She licked her lips, curious to know more about him now that she'd spilled her guts. "Did you ever fall for the wrong person, Ryder?"

"Not with the same kind of drama as your recent relationship, but I've gone out with a few women who would fall into the category of *what were you thinking*?"

"Really. That's interesting. Tell me about one of them."

"I don't really remember."

"Yes, you do. Come on, I've already given you my talk of shame. You can share something."

"All right. I dated one woman I thought was single, but she turned out to be married. And her husband was a Navy commander."

"Ooh, that is not good, Ryder."

"Definitely not good," he agreed.

"How did you find out?"

"We were at a restaurant and she left her phone on the table when she went to use the restroom. I saw a text message flash across the screen. I read it before I realized what I was doing. It was from her husband, asking her why she wasn't at her mother's house when she'd told him she was going there."

"What happened next?"

"I confronted her. She said she was bored and

unhappy and that her husband was thirteen years older than her and she just wanted to have some fun. I told her we were done and I immediately left."

"Did you get in trouble with the commander?"

"No. I thought she might try to do something to hurt me, because she seemed a little vindictive when I ditched her in the restaurant, but I guess she couldn't turn me in without turning herself in, so that was that. Now, I make sure to look for rings and tan lines."

"I can understand being wary after that. Did you like her? Did you love her?"

He shook his head. "No, I didn't love her, and after I learned that she'd been lying to me, I realized I didn't like her all that much, either."

"It's funny how feelings can change in an instant when someone's real face is unmasked. But then you have to ask yourself, is there anyone out there who isn't wearing a mask? Will I always be surprised or shocked or hurt by some revelation? How can I really trust my instincts, when they were so wrong before?" As the words flew out of her mouth, she knew she was revealing way too much, but it was too late to take anything back.

Ryder placed his hand over hers, where it rested on the table. His fingers were warm, his touch both reassuring and unsettling. "You'll find a way to trust again—when it's the right person. You'll know what to look for. You'll know if you're seeing them for who they are or who you want them to be. And I'm not so sure that it's other people who are wearing the mask. Sometimes, I think it's us. We see what we want to see, what we need to see."

"I never thought of it that way."

"It's easier to blame the other person."

"True, but Franco is to blame for a lot of the problems in my life. He's not innocent in this. Even if I didn't see him for who he is, he still did bad things."

"Exactly. Now you're starting to take responsibility *only* for what you did, not for what he did." His fingers tightened around hers. "We have to own what's ours, but we don't have to carry what isn't ours. It took me a long time to figure that out."

She wanted to ask him exactly how he'd figured it out when the oven timer went off, and she was reminded of the fruit tart she'd put in the oven before they'd sat down. "Dessert," she said, feeling a little cold as Ryder let go of her hand. "I hope you're still hungry."

"Not right this second. Can it cool while we take a walk? We still have a lot of things to talk about."

"A walk is a good idea." Leaving the intimacy of Ryder's cozy kitchen would be a good way to start putting some distance between them. She was starting to feel way too close to this man.

As Ryder had just reminded her, it was easy to see what she wanted to see. And right now, she was seeing Ryder as one of the sexiest, most interesting men she'd met in a long time, and that was more than a little disconcerting.

Six

After putting the tart on the counter to cool, Bailey grabbed her jacket while Ryder shrugged on his coat, and they walked outside together. The air was cold, but the earlier clouds had parted, letting more moonlight and stars shine through. However, she was still happy that Ryder had grabbed a flashlight before they left the house, since the land next to his home was undeveloped.

"I don't know this area very well," she said, as they walked across the lawn and through the trees. "You'll have to lead."

"Happy to," he said, shining the light on the dirt path in front of them. "I know this part of town very well. My grandmother had her restaurant a half mile from here—Veronica's. Do you remember the place? Did you ever go there? Or was it off-limits because it was owned by a Westbrook?"

"I remember Veronica's. We only went there once. I thought we didn't go there because it was expensive, but maybe it was because it was owned by your grandmother."

"So why the one time? What was the occasion?"

"It was a celebration for my mom. She had just gotten the part in the show *Mother May I*. She was leaving for Hollywood in the morning, and her friends threw her a party at Veronica's. The restaurant was so beautiful—rich and luxurious. I remember crystals and candles and the prettiest plates. I felt like I'd stepped into another world. It was definitely not like the diner."

"My grandmother wanted people to feel like they were in a completely different reality when they stepped inside her restaurant. It might have been located in small-town America, but she wanted it to feel like it could be in New York or Paris. To be honest, I think it was a little pretentious, but that's the Westbrook way," he said dryly.

She liked that he could be honest about his family, even though she didn't think Ryder was pretentious at all. In fact, he was much more down-to-earth than she would have imagined he'd be.

"Tell me about your mom," Ryder continued. "I know she left to become a famous actress and that Zane and Adam weren't too thrilled about it. Since your parents ended up getting divorced, I'm guessing your dad didn't like it much, either."

"At first, we were all excited. It was fun to think of my mom being on TV. We never really imagined that the show could turn into a huge hit, that it would run for eight years, that our mother, who had in fact left her own kids and husband behind, would become television's perfect mom. It was weirdly ironic."

"Why didn't you all move to LA with her?"

"My dad is a proud man. He didn't want to live off his wife's salary; he had the restaurant to run, and we were all in school. In the beginning, they both thought she'd be back in a few months. But months turned into years, and my mom's dreams kept coming true. She'd put aside being an actress for a long time. She'd spent years raising Adam, Zane, and me, and when this opportunity came up, she wanted it, and she took it. And no one was very happy about it. Were we the selfish ones, or was it her? Who knows?"

"It sounds complicated. How did you feel about it?"

She let out a sigh. "So many things. Excited, angry, sad, lonely, unsure... I was eleven when she left. I was coming into a really hard age. It was difficult to be without my mom, to be living with all guys—all clueless guys."

He gave her a faint smile. "I can't even imagine."

"They tried, but they didn't know what to do. My dad was angry with my mom, so he was caught up in that. Thank God Brenda was around. She was my mom's friend. She worked at the diner. She felt like a second mother to me. She took me to do all the things young girls need to do and that my father was embarrassed to even talk about."

"Did you see your mom at all?"

"I saw her quite a bit the first few years. I spent a couple of weeks each summer with her. My brothers were older, so they didn't go as often as I did. My mom's life was glamorous and beautiful—celebrities everywhere, money no object. It was a vastly different experience than living in Eagle's Ridge. But my mom was busy a lot of the time, too. She didn't just have the TV show; she had lots of other opportunities. Soon, she was making movies and traveling to film festivals. When I was in LA, I spent more time with the housekeeper than with her. Eventually, we all realized she wasn't coming back. As much as she claimed to love us all, she had a life she loved more. By the time my parents divorced, the boys were grown and out of the house, and while my parents shared custody of me, my mom didn't fight to see me more than was convenient to her."

"You must have been hurt and angry."

"I was, but I still loved her. And as I got older, I started to see there was another side. My dad could have moved for her. It really shouldn't have been all on her to keep us together. But maybe I'm not being fair to my dad when I say that, because he was there for me, and she wasn't. It's complicated."

"Is she in your life now?"

"Not really. We occasionally text, or she'll invite me to something, but I don't go, and our communication dies as quickly as it starts. She remarried a few years ago. She has her own life, and I have mine." She paused. "I think my mom's leaving spurred on my cooking career, though. My dad was so busy at the diner after she left, and he was so caught up in his pain that he kind of overlooked my brothers and me. I started cooking dinner, because I was tired of always having to go to the diner to get food, and then one day my dad started coming home for dinner, and somehow we found our way back to being a family again—even without her."

"That was because of you."

"No one gives me credit for that, but yes it was because of me. And I don't know what it is about you that makes me want to talk so much, Ryder."

He smiled. "Is it me or just being home again? It makes you think about the life you used to lead. At least, coming back here has done that to me."

She was happy not to be the only one feeling nostalgic. "I suppose it is partly that and also because I feel like I'm facing a transition point. I was on one road the last two years and I crashed into a brick wall. I have to back up and decide if I want to take another road or fix that one."

"What are you leaning toward?"

"Picking another road. I could never trust Franco again. I guess I have to decide if that road goes back to New York or somewhere else. I have to say having to choose where I want to be reminds me of my mother and the choices she made between family and ambition."

"Have you ever talked to her about it?"

"Not as an adult, no."

"Maybe you should—if you think she'll give you an answer, of course. If I asked my mother anything more serious than what's for dinner, she'd start panicking, reaching for her not-so-secret stash of cigarettes or another glass of wine. And then she would change the subject and that would be the end of that."

She shot him a quick look, hearing a touch of anger in his voice. "So, life isn't always wonderful at the Westbrook's?"

He uttered a short, harsh laugh. "It *is* wonderful, because no one ever challenges the idea that it's not. My parents don't talk about feelings. Neither does my grandfather. If you have a problem, you keep it to yourself, and you solve it on your own. That's the way it works."

"Sounds a little rough."

"Rough makes you tough—another truism from

my grandfather. Have you ever spoken to him?"

"No, I've probably only seen him a few times in my life or in the local paper when he was being praised for something. Is your grandfather well?"

"Yes. His body might be moving a little slower, but his mind is still sharp." He pulled some bushes away from the path. "Watch your step."

"Thanks." As she moved past the bushes, she got a great view of the river. The path they were on was about six feet above the water, but she was reminded again of how high the river was running. "I guess there was a lot of rain this winter. The river is running high."

"Yes, there's some concern about flooding if we continue to get more storms, but hopefully that won't happen."

"Hopefully not."

"Your brothers are probably happy about the river level. It should make for a better season for A To Z Watersports."

"That's true."

"Do you raft and kayak like your brothers?"

"I did when I was younger. Adam and Zane and I were river rats. We did everything we could on the river. But it's been awhile for me." She paused, spying a building to the left and up a small hill. "Is that the restaurant?"

"Yes. That's Veronica's."

"Can we take a closer look?"

"Sure."

"When did it close?" she asked, following him up the hill.

"When my grandmother died twelve years ago. My grandfather couldn't bear to sell it or rent it out, so he just locked the doors, and it has sat empty ever since."

"That seems a shame."

"He couldn't stand the idea of someone else running Veronica's or changing it into something else. It was her passion. She didn't open the restaurant until she was in her fifties. It was something she'd always thought about doing, but she wasn't a chef, so she wasn't quite sure how to get started. Finally, my grandfather told her to stop complaining about there not being any good food in town and open up a restaurant, so she did. She worked with several different chefs over the next twenty-five years, and she loved planning the menus, hosting events, being the special place people went to for their special meals. In the last few years of her life, she was barely in the restaurant, but she still kept an eye on the menu, and she would occasionally drop in unexpectedly to make sure her standards were being met."

"She sounds like a dedicated restauranteur. Not all restaurant owners care that much."

"She was definitely devoted to the restaurant and my grandfather was devoted to her. The only time in my life that I ever saw him blink back a tear was when she died. That's it. And it lasted about two seconds. But they were married for over fifty years."

"My grandparents were married that long, too," she said, wondering what that would feel like. She couldn't even imagine.

"So, here it is," Ryder said, as they stepped onto the brick patio that had once given diners a beautiful view of the river during hot summer nights.

"I don't remember this patio."

"You probably came in the winter."

Her gaze swept across the building: the peeling paint, the fading shutters, and the vine-colored walls. It saddened her to see the restaurant all closed up, a shell of its once vibrant self. "It feels like it's waiting to be rediscovered. To have another time to shine." Excitement ran down her spine as an unexpected idea began to form. "Eagle's Ridge could use a really good restaurant. This patio, with the song of the river, the moonlight through the trees—it's perfect. It's inspiring."

"You're getting a little carried away. My grandfather will never sell it."

"What if it was partly an homage to Veronica's but more modern, more organic..." She spun around as her brain began to shimmer with ideas. "I could see a dozen tables out here in the bright afternoon sun and then at night, the restaurant could become more elegant, luxurious, expensive, but not too expensive. We'd want the locals to come, but we'd also want to appeal to the tourists."

"We? Who's going to run this imaginary restaurant?" he queried, giving her a pointed look. "You?"

"Well...I don't know."

"I thought you said you were just visiting, that your life is somewhere else."

"It was somewhere else." She knew it was crazy to contemplate coming back to Eagle's Ridge. The culinary world was not here, and she'd left her hometown a long time ago to pursue that world, to be a force within it.

"This seems like something you need to think about, Bailey. You'll never find the acclaim, the customers, the money in a restaurant here in Eagle's

Ridge, not like you'd find in New York or Los Angeles or San Francisco. Isn't that the dream you left Eagle's Ridge to chase?"

"That was the dream. But dreams change." The more she thought about it, the more it made sense. Sure, there were voices in her head screaming caution, telling her not to throw New York away just because of Franco and her bad experience there, but there were other voices suggesting that perhaps she'd always been meant to come back here.

"And hurt fades," he said pointedly. "You might feel differently in a few days or even a few weeks."

"I might," she admitted.

"Besides, my grandfather won't sell the restaurant. It means too much to him."

"I guess I can't blame him for wanting to hang on to something that reminds him of his wife. Maybe he's not as soulless as I've heard he is."

"He did love Veronica," Ryder said.

She walked across the patio and sat down on the low brick wall overlooking the moonlit water. "This place feels magical," she murmured. "I don't usually see the river from this side."

Ryder sat down next to her. "Sometimes it's good to change your perspective."

"Not just good—important." She glanced over at him, then brought up the subject they'd been dancing around all night. "I don't know how to help you, Ryder; I really don't. Your grandfather doesn't want to sell his restaurant, even though it's been closed for more than a decade. And my grandfather's land means everything to him. They're both stubborn old men."

"Who are living in the past."

"They're in their nineties—that's a lot of past to

try to move them away from."

"Maybe it's about their legacies then," he suggested. "I have to try, Bailey."

"Are you sure this is where you want to be?" It was the same question he'd asked her, and she needed to know. "You've been back here longer than me, but only by a few months. Are you sure you won't find this town really slow and quiet after all the action you've seen? You're a soldier—a warrior."

"I was a soldier, but that part of my life is over. And it won't be that slow or quiet around here if I can do what I want to do at the airport."

"Maybe not." She gave him a thoughtful look. "But I feel like you didn't just come back to Eagle's Ridge to expand the airport, bring more tourists to town, or fly search and rescue for reckless hikers."

He tipped his head. "I suppose there's a bit more to it than that."

"Like what?"

He didn't answer right away, then said, "When my helo was shot down, it was the first time I really thought my number might be up. And you know what came into my mind?"

"Home?"

He nodded, turning to look into her eyes. "In my head, I saw this river and the Blue Mountains. I saw the past I'd run away from, and I made a promise to myself that if I survived, I'd come back. I'd take care of unfinished business."

The deep emotion in his voice wasn't completely explained by his words. "Is it the town or your family that you're not finished with?"

He gave her a faint smile. "Both. But it's also myself. I left here when I was eighteen. I didn't think I could be who I wanted to be in this town. And at the time I couldn't. But a lot has changed since then. Eagle's Ridge means more to me now, because there was a moment when I didn't think I'd ever see this beautiful place again. I want to be somewhere that's growing, that's hopeful, where there's a future. And the people in this town, with the exception of our grandparents, do work together."

She was touched by his words and ached a little at the pain in his voice, her mind imagining the terror he must have gone through thinking that his life might end. It really made her recent disaster seem a lot less important.

Impulsively, she put a hand on his shoulder. "I'm so glad you survived, Ryder. That you had a chance to come back."

"Me, too," he said, a husky note in his voice.

She swallowed hard as their gazes clung together, as the whisper of his breath brushed against her cheek. He was so close, and she wanted him closer...

He seemed to want that, too.

His head lowered.

She licked her suddenly dry lips.

He sucked in a quick breath and then his hand came around the back of her neck, and he pulled her toward him, his mouth coming down on hers with a hunger, a force, that matched the rushing blood in her veins.

Surrounded by the cool mountain air, Ryder's lips were smoking hot, and the electricity between them added a reckless danger to the moment. Her brain was racing to keep up with her desire, but it was a losing battle.

It didn't make sense that she was kissing Ryder.

But who needed sense when there were all these wonderful, glorious, shivery feelings, when every nerve ending had come alive, when they couldn't stop at one kiss or two or three…when all she could think about was that there were too many clothes between them?

Finally, a desperate need for air broke them apart. Their breaths mixed together in a hot cloud between them.

But the heat was shattered by a cold drop of water on her face.

She blinked in confusion as another drop landed close to her eye.

Rain!

She suddenly realized it was raining. There had been moonlight just a minute ago, but now there were thick, swirling clouds overhead and a misty rain starting to come down.

"We should go back," Ryder said, jumping to his feet.

He extended his hand, and she took it, sliding off the low wall. They jogged down the hill, their pace increasing as the rain got harder. Once again, she found herself slipping and sliding on muddy ground, but Ryder never let go of her hand. He wouldn't let her fall, and while he was just being a gentleman, it still put a knot in her throat. A lot of men would have let her fend for herself, and she was more than capable of doing that, but every now and then it was nice to have someone else looking out for her.

By the time they reached Ryder's front porch, they were both soaking wet, the skies having opened up with a ridiculously hard downpour. She pushed wet strands of hair off her face while Ryder shook off the water clinging to his jacket.

"Where did that come from?" she asked.

"Maybe the universe thought we needed a cold shower," he said with a grin. "That was some kiss, Bailey."

She couldn't help but smile back at him. "It was." She paused as thunder rocked the air followed almost immediately by a streak of lightning. "I didn't think it was enough to do that, but maybe…"

He laughed. "Let's go inside. We can have dessert."

She had a feeling if she went inside, dessert was going to involve their naked bodies and not the delicious tart she'd made earlier. And as much as that tantalizing thought made the butterflies in her stomach zip around with anticipation, her brain was telling her to slow the hell down.

"I think I should go home," she said, feeling both proud of her willpower and ridiculously disappointed.

Ryder's smile faded. "Nothing will happen that you don't want to happen."

"I know that. I just don't know what I want to happen," she said honestly.

"Fair enough. So, let's just have some of that tart you made."

"I'm still full."

"You're sure I can't talk you into dessert?"

He could talk her into a lot more than that, which was exactly why she needed to leave. "Another time," she said. "I just need to grab my bag, but I don't want to drip all over your floors and furniture."

"I'll get it for you."

"It's on the kitchen counter."

He disappeared into the house, returning with her

purse a moment later. "Is this all you need?"

"That's it." She paused. "I'm going to help you, Ryder—with my grandfather."

Relief and surprise flashed across his face. "Seriously?"

"Yes. Because it's a worthy cause. I'll set up a meeting. I can't guarantee he'll show up but I'll do my best. I think it's a ridiculous long shot."

He smiled. "Maybe. But there's nothing better than making something happen that everyone thinks can't be done."

"You could fail, Ryder."

"Not trying would be worse."

His words touched off a wave of self-recrimination, and suddenly she was asking herself why she hadn't fought harder against Franco and his lies. Why hadn't she fought for her reputation? Why had she run away? "You must think I'm an awful coward," she murmured.

"Why would you say that, Bailey?"

"Because I didn't stay in New York and fight for my good name."

He gave her a long look. "I don't think you're a coward because you came home. Maybe deep down you knew the relationship—the restaurant—wasn't worth fighting for."

"You might be giving me more credit than I deserve."

"I don't think so. But bottom line—it doesn't matter what other people believe; it only matters what you think. It's your life, your choices. Only you have to understand them."

"I appreciate you saying that. I might be a little more swayed by what people think of me than you are."

"Well, I think you're one of the most interesting, beautiful, and talented women I've ever met."

She drew in a quick breath as his words started the flutters once again. "Even if that's a line, I like it."

"It's not a line. And I'm not saying it to get you on my side. What happened a few minutes ago—that wasn't about the land. You know that, right?"

She nodded. "I know that."

"Good. Why don't you come by the airfield tomorrow? I can show you exactly what I want to do. That might help you figure out a plan to get your grandfather on board."

More time with Ryder seemed like a fabulous idea. "All right. I told my dad I'd help out in the diner this week, but I'll see what I can do. Maybe after lunch, when it gets slow for a few hours."

"Perfect. We have a plan."

"You like plans, don't you?"

"I do. I've never been an impulsive person."

"Well, I am the complete opposite. I usually jump off the cliff and figure out a plan on the way down, which is probably why I'm in the mess I'm in."

"You're going to land on your feet, Bailey." He gave her a smile that washed over her in a warm wave, creating more tingly feelings and a wish that she hadn't said no to his offer for dessert. "I also think we're going to make a good team."

Being on Ryder's team seemed like a great idea. And as she dashed through the rain to her car, she couldn't help thinking it was really too bad she was off men…

Seven

—➤➤◄◄◄—

Bailey entered the kitchen at No Man's Land a little before seven on Friday. Her dad had gotten in at six to accept some early-morning deliveries from the local baker and vegetable supplier, so he was already up to his elbows in pancake and waffle batter.

He gave her a quick look. "So, you're really going to help out this morning?"

"I said I would," she reminded him. They hadn't spoken much since she'd arrived in town, but when he'd asked her how she felt about giving him a hand at the diner for a few days, she hadn't been able to say no. His normal prep cook was taking a few days off since his wife had just had a baby, so her dad was short-handed.

She put her purse in the storeroom and grabbed an apron, then returned to the kitchen. "What do you want me on?"

"Eggs and omelets, and no fancy stuff that's not on the menu," he said, giving her a pointed look. "You'll get everyone's hopes up and then they'll be disappointed when you go back to New York."

"I'll stick to the menu." She opened the large refrigerator door to check on the egg supply and the other vegetables she would need to cook her father's dishes. While her dad didn't like to experiment a lot, he served up deliciously seasoned, perfectly cooked food with every order, and now that she knew so much more about the restaurant business than she had as a kid, she appreciated his consistency.

"Good morning," Brenda said cheerfully, as she entered the kitchen. "It's nice to have you back, Bailey."

She wanted to say it was nice to be there, but she still wasn't quite sure how she felt about being in a restaurant kitchen again. Cooking for Ryder at his house had been one thing. But she was about to put her skills on display for a lot of friends and neighbors, some of whom might not trust her cooking anymore.

"I don't know if this is a good idea," she said. "You've been nice not to ask, but I suspect you've both heard some rumors about me."

"None of which I believe are true," Brenda said firmly. "You're an incredible cook."

"And you're very careful with ingredients and preparation," her dad put in. "Something else happened in that restaurant to make those people sick, but I know you didn't have anything to do with it. If you had, you would have stood up and said so. You're not a coward. You've always taken responsibility when you did something wrong."

Her eyes blurred at her dad's strong words. "It means a lot to me that you both believe that. I guess my secret wasn't so secret after all."

"It's not difficult to believe in you," Brenda said. "We know you."

"And we love you," her dad finished.

"Thanks. That means a lot to me. I didn't prepare the food that made the customers sick. If I had been on that dish, I would have checked the fish. And I would have taken responsibility if I had done it."

"Of course you would have," her father said with a nod. "Now, what's happening with your job?"

"Well, I was fired, so there is no job."

"He fired you for what wasn't your mistake?" her dad asked with anger in his voice. "How can he do that?"

"It doesn't matter. I don't want to work for him ever again. I need to start over, find a new path, get my confidence back." She knew she needed to say something to her father that he probably wouldn't like, but she didn't want there to be any more misunderstandings. "I know that you'd still like me to consider taking over No Man's Land one day, Dad, but I don't think I can do that. I feel badly, because it's the family business, and God knows neither Adam nor Zane could run this place. But whether I go back to New York or somewhere else, it's time for me to do something on my own. I don't know exactly what it's going to be, but I'm tired of working on other people's dreams. I want to work on my own."

"I have known for a long time that your destiny is not this diner," her father said with complete understanding in his warm blue eyes. "But you can always work here until you figure out what you want. I'm just glad you came home, Bailey. Not only have we missed you, but I think you need to remember who you are. Eagle's Ridge is a good place to do that."

"You're the best," she said, giving him a hug.

"Only when I give you what you want," he

teased.

She smiled back at him. "Even when you don't."

"You'll find your way," Brenda added. "You've never been short on big ideas, Bailey."

"I just have to make sure the big ideas are the right ones."

Brenda turned away as they heard the diner door open and a group of customers enter the restaurant. "Looks like it's time for you two to start cooking."

For the next several hours, the kitchen was slammed with orders. Bailey found herself reveling in the fast pace, the hot kitchen, the challenge of making sure every dish was perfect.

Brenda and a young woman named Mandy took the orders out to the diners as fast as they could get them done, and everything ran very smoothly, but Bailey shouldn't have been surprised about that. Her father and Brenda had been working together for a long time, and they seemed to know what each other needed without anyone having to say anything.

The breakfast rush turned into a lunch rush, and it wasn't until almost two that Bailey had a minute to think about anything but food. However, as the crowd in the diner thinned out, her thoughts turned to Ryder and her promise to come by the airfield. Just thinking about seeing him again sent a shiver down her spine. She'd spun some lovely fantasies in her head last night, but she couldn't or shouldn't go there. At least, not right now…

She had a lot of things to figure out and throwing Ryder into the mix would not be smart. She didn't even know how long she'd be in Eagle's Ridge. Starting something was a bad idea, but there was a part of her that wondered if they hadn't started something already.

Still, she had promised to help him with her grandfather, and it would be helpful to see the land in question. Taking off her apron, she hung it on a hook and told her father she was going out for a while.

"No worries," he returned as he cleaned the grill. "Have fun."

She slung her bag over her shoulder and walked into the diner. There was only one older couple sitting by the window, finishing up their salads and soups as they looked out at the river. After last night's heavy rain, the sun was shining again, but the river was even higher than it had been the day before.

"Taking a break?" Brenda asked, as she ran a cloth over the counter in front of her. "It was like old times having you in the kitchen today, Bailey."

"It felt like I never left, once I remembered that Master Guns meant eggs," she added dryly. "Is there any coffee?"

"There is," Brenda said. "Help yourself."

She grabbed a to-go cup and filled it with coffee. "So, how are you, Brenda?"

"I'm fine. Nothing new. Life goes on."

Brenda had always had an easygoing and caring personality, never letting her personal problems or feelings affect how she did her job. And it wasn't as if Brenda had always had it easy. Her military husband had been killed in action almost ten years ago, but Brenda had taken only a few days off before coming back to work, saying she needed to be busy.

"No Eagle's Ridge gossip to share?" she pressed, taking a sip of her coffee.

"Nothing particularly interesting."

Brenda's gaze drifted toward the kitchen, and

there was something a little off in her response, but she couldn't quite figure out what it was. "Everything okay with you and my dad?" she asked.

"Of course," Brenda said quickly, looking a little flustered by the question. "We're fine. We're always fine. Why do you ask?"

"I don't know. It just seems like there's something on your mind."

"Well…" Brenda began. "It's not a big deal, but I've been thinking about taking a class at the community college."

"Really? What kind of class?"

"Photography. It's silly because everyone takes pictures on their phone now. It's not like I need to learn how to use a fancy camera or if I should even spend the money to get one. It's not practical."

"Sometimes it's good to be impractical, and I don't think it's silly at all. When are the classes?"

"Wednesday nights, which is another problem, because I work most Wednesday nights."

"So, change your day off; I'm sure my dad wouldn't mind."

"Maybe not. But then again, he's not big on change."

She supposed that was true. Her dad was great, but he was quite predictable. Still, he appreciated Brenda so much for all she'd done, not just at the diner but by being a mother to his kids. "My dad would want to support you. Let's ask him now."

"No, not now," Brenda said with a quick shake of her head. "I need to think about it a little more. I'm just feeling restless. Next week it's going to be ten years since Doug was killed. I can't believe it's been that long. Sometimes it feels like yesterday, and other times it feels like a million years ago."

"I'm sure it's always going to be difficult."

"Always," Brenda agreed. "Anyway, let's talk about you. You seemed to be having an interesting conversation with Ryder Westbrook in here yesterday."

She felt a rush of heat warm her cheeks, which drew Brenda's attention.

"Well, well," Brenda murmured. "Did I touch a nerve?"

"No, you didn't touch a nerve. Ryder helped me out with something the other day, and so I told him I would pay him back."

"What did he do for you and, more importantly, what are you going to do for him?"

She cast a quick glance around the restaurant to make sure Zane hadn't silently come in while they were talking. "I kind of let Gambler out of the house Wednesday night when I was watching him for Zane. Ryder came by the house to see my dad and wound up helping me with Gambler, but you can't tell Zane. I will never hear the end of it. It will be the goldfish episode all over again."

Brenda smiled. "Your secret is safe with me. But that doesn't explain what you're doing with Ryder."

"He wants to expand the airfield, and he needs Tucker land to do it. He wants me to smooth the way with Grandpa."

"That's going to take a great deal of smoothing," Brenda said with a frown. "He's a Westbrook."

"I know, but he thinks the feud is stupid and should have ended years ago, and I can't disagree. Plus, I think a bigger airfield would allow larger planes to land, which helps all of us." She paused. "Do you think Grandpa could be swayed?"

"I don't know, Bailey. He's not one for changing his mind and getting older hasn't made him any less stubborn. When it comes to Westbrooks, he doesn't think with his head; it's all heart."

"I agree. I told Ryder that, but he wants me to see the land in question."

A gleam entered Brenda's eyes. "So, you're going to see Ryder."

"Yes, but it's business." She paused as her phone buzzed. Looking at the screen, she expected to see a text from a NY friend or some foodie reporter, but it was from her mom. She frowned and opened the message, her stomach turning over uneasily as she read the short text. "I can't believe I have to deal with this now," she muttered. "As if I don't have enough to worry about."

"Is something wrong?"

"I don't know. My mom wants me to call her. I just don't know if I can deal with her right now."

"Maybe she has good news," Brenda said, her expression carefully neutral.

Brenda had always been careful not to criticize her former friend, even though Brenda had been on the front lines of the terrible fallout between her mom, her dad, and the rest of her family.

"She doesn't usually share bad news. With my mom, it's always about how wonderful her life is. I don't think she would ever want us to think she'd made the wrong decision by leaving us to take a television role."

"She hurt all of you terribly, and I don't know how she ever walked away from you and your brothers or your father. Men like him don't come around very often..." Brenda's gaze drifted once again toward the kitchen pass.

The odd look on Brenda's face made Bailey wonder. Brenda and her dad had always been the best of friends and they ran the restaurant together, but was there more between them?

Brenda turned back to her. "But your mom was an actress before she married your dad and she gave that up for a long time to be a wife and a mother. Maybe it was her turn to have a chance at her dream."

"I do understand her decisions a little better now that I'm grown up," she admitted, "now that I have dreams of my own. But my mom didn't do it right. She could have commuted or found a way to merge her dreams with her family. Why did it have to be a choice? All or nothing? That's what I don't understand."

"It's easier to see other choices when you're looking back. Are you going to answer her text?"

She drew in a breath. "Later. Don't mention it to Dad. It will just upset him."

"I won't."

"I'll be back before the dinner rush."

"Take your time. And say hello to Ryder for me."

"I will, but you can get that little smile off your face. I'm just helping out a friend."

"You and Ryder are friends now?"

She let out a little sigh. "Honestly, I have no idea what we are."

The Eagle's Ridge Airfield had been Ryder's home away from home when he was growing up. He'd started taking flight lessons when he was fourteen years old. He'd gotten his pilot's license before his driver's license. He'd found joy, adventure, escape in the sky, and he didn't just want to keep the airport going; he wanted to make it better for generations to come.

He swiveled in his office chair and looked out at the property. The 220-acre airport was owned by the city of Eagle's Ridge, but it had been managed by David Bennett, since its inception. David retired as general manager fifteen years ago and turned the job over to his son Greg, who had been working there since his twenties.

But now Greg was sixty. His two kids were grown and living far away from Eagle's Ridge, and Greg and his wife wanted to travel. When Greg had heard Ryder was back in town, he'd reached out to him about taking over airport operations.

He'd brushed the idea aside at first. He was a pilot, not a desk jockey, but once he'd come back to the airfield, and looked at all the ways the airport could be expanded, which would not only bring more tourists and money into town but would also allow them to provide better support for search and rescue and wildfires, he'd known this was what he was meant to do next.

Getting up, he moved closer to the window, looking out at the runway, the heliport, the half-dozen hangars that could be rented out if they had more aircraft requiring space. In his mind, he could see a bustling airport, far different than the sleepy airfield it was now.

A knock turned him around, and his heart jumped at the sight of Bailey Tucker. Wearing skinny jeans, boots, and a dark-green wool coat over a cream-colored top, her blonde hair flowing loosely around her shoulders, her light-blue eyes bright and gleaming, she looked even prettier than the image he'd carried around in his head since last night.

"I'm glad you came," he said.

"I said I would, and I have a few hours before I have to get back to the diner for dinner prep. I have to say I haven't been out here in years. I always fly into Seattle or Spokane and drive from there."

"Which is what I'm trying to change. I want to make it a lot easier for everyone to get here."

"Do you worry it will bring too many people into town? There's a certain charm about the isolation of Eagle's Ridge."

"Charm doesn't pay bills, and a busy airport will bring in jobs. If you decide to open your own restaurant, you'll be looking for customers, too."

She smiled. "I agree. Do you want to show me around?"

"I do, but the best way to really see the airport is from the sky."

She stiffened. "You want to take me up in a plane?"

"A helicopter."

"Oh, I don't know. That sounds kind of scary."

"It's quite fun, and I'm a very good pilot. You'll be safe, Bailey."

"I'm sure you are good, but maybe we should just walk around."

"Come on. I promise to bring you back in one piece, and I think you'll enjoy it." He paused, giving her a thoughtful look. "I know you're not a fearful person. You grew up whitewater rafting with your brothers. So why the hesitation?"

She gave a helpless shrug. "I don't know. You're right. I used to be a lot braver than I seem to be now. I will go in the helicopter with you."

"Excellent. I've already double-checked our ride in the hopes that you would say yes, so I'm ready to go if you are."

"I guess I am."

As Ryder reached for his jacket, David Bennett ambled into the office. At ninety-three, David had lost a few inches of height, putting him at about five foot seven now, with a wiry frame, olive skin, white hair, still sharp and curious brown eyes, and notably large ears that had given him the nickname Dumbo. Those big ears had ironically started to fail him in recent years, making every conversation more of a shouting match.

While David no longer worked at the airport, he still stopped by at least three to four times a week to check up on things—as he liked to say—but mostly he just enjoyed being there, watching the action, even if he couldn't direct it anymore.

"Well, well, well," David said, his gaze on Bailey. "If it isn't the prettiest girl in town."

"You always say that," Bailey said, giving David a hug. "It is good to see you. How are you?"

"Getting younger every day," David said with a laugh.

"I can see that."

"What are you doing here?" he asked.

"Ryder is going to take me for a ride."

"He's going to make you his bride?" David echoed, looking confused. "You two getting married?"

"No, no," Bailey said quickly, speaking more

loudly. "He's going to take me up in the helicopter for a ride."

"You need to turn up your hearing aid," Ryder said dryly.

"I can hear just fine," David retorted. "You tell Bailey about your plans?"

"Yes. I'm going to show her where the extended runway will go before we talk to Max." He paused, his gaze narrowing. He'd asked David not to share his plan with Max Tucker until he formulated his thoughts, but the two men spent time together, having dinner at least once a week. "You haven't said anything to Max, have you?"

"Nope. Last thing I'm looking to do these days is set a spark to the dynamite keg that has always been Max Tucker," David said.

"Do you think Ryder's plan is a good one?" Bailey asked.

"Absolutely. But Max won't sell one inch of his land to the city, because everyone knows the city is run by the Westbrooks. Sorry, Ryder. But that's the way he thinks."

He shrugged. "No apologies necessary."

"But you would be in favor of the plan?" Bailey persisted. "I feel like my grandfather should hear that from you, because you've run the airport your whole life. You know what it needs better than anyone."

"I know it needs someone younger than me, someone with more fight," David said, giving him a pointed look. "I think Ryder is up for the challenge."

"It seems more like an unsurmountable obstacle than a challenge," Bailey commented.

"Well, let's take a ride," Ryder put in, not wanting her to change her mind before he had a chance to show her his plans. "We'll keep thinking about how to approach Max."

"Have fun," David said, waving them on. "I'll watch over things around here."

Ryder didn't bother to say that the airport was already under the careful watch of three other employees; David liked to feel useful.

They made their way downstairs and through the terminal area, which housed the flight school office, a small waiting room, a coffee/deli kiosk and the business offices.

As they exited the building and headed to the heliport, Jason, one of the older teenagers who worked at the airport part-time so he could pay for flight lessons, came over to help them get set up with headphones and microphones so they'd be able to communicate once they were in the air. Then Bailey climbed into the passenger seat while he slipped behind the controls and went through his final pre-check.

A quick glance at Bailey showed tension on her face, so he gave her a reassuring smile. "You're going to love this."

"I hope so."

"You can trust me, Bailey."

"I'm counting on that."

The look in her eyes made him realize that trust for her was probably not a particularly easy thing to come by these days. He was not going to be the man to let her down.

Eight

Bailey knew Ryder was an accomplished pilot, but she still couldn't quite shake the waves of anxiety running through her body. She'd never been comfortable giving up control, whether it was in the kitchen or anywhere else in her life. But she was even less comfortable now, having been so recently burned by someone she'd thought she loved and who she'd believed was trustworthy. But this wasn't about love, and Ryder didn't owe her anything except a safe and uneventful ride.

Drawing in a breath, she prepared herself for takeoff, which was smoother and less stomach-churning than she would have thought. She didn't have a problem flying in airplanes, but she felt much more exposed in the helicopter. There was more movement, more air, more…everything.

She suddenly realized that it wasn't just fear running through her when Ryder took them up over the tree line and flew toward town; it was also excitement.

"I thought you were just going to show me the

runway," she said.

"When we go back. Feeling okay?"

"Actually, I feel great." She was surprised to admit it, but it was true.

"Good," he said, a smile curving his sexy mouth. "I knew you'd like it."

She didn't just like it; she liked *him*. But she wasn't going to tell him that.

She turned her gaze toward the vista unfolding before them. Tall trees and the running river gave way to houses and roads. She could see homes tucked into the hillier side of the river where she'd grown up; it was a vantage point she'd never had before.

"Your grandfather's place is through those trees," Ryder said. "And there's your dad's house."

"It looks even smaller from up here." With all the trees, hillsides and dense foliage, it was clear to see why the other side of the river had been much easier to develop.

Sentinel Bridge came into view, with No Man's Land and the boathouse for A To Z Watersports beyond. She almost wished someone was outside, so she could wave hello. On the other hand, flying around with Ryder was bound to bring up all kinds of questions, so maybe it was just as well no one was outside.

She looked off to the right as Ryder flew them toward the downtown area, where retail shops, restaurants, markets and small inns dotted the landscape. She could see the cluster of schools, the library, the parks with tennis and basketball courts, softball and soccer fields—all the places that marked moments of her youth.

On the Westbrook side of the river, the houses

were much grander with a lot more acreage per plot.

"Where's the house you grew up in?" she asked Ryder.

"Coming up," he said, pointing ahead of them. "It's the two-story house with the low brick wall."

"And the tennis court in the back?"

"Yes. It doubled as a basketball court when I was growing up. I never got into tennis, even though both my parents play. The house is rented out now. My parents moved in with my grandfather eight years ago." A moment later, he added. "My grandfather's house is that big white colonial."

"That's right. It's the *Gone with the Wind* house."

"Yes. That was my grandmother's favorite book and movie."

Seeing where Ryder had grown up, reminded her of how very different their childhoods had been.

"Now, I'm going to show you my favorite view," he said, a note of excitement in his voice. He made a sweeping turn and flew back over the town, heading toward the Blue Mountains and Eagle's Ridge.

They didn't speak for the next few minutes, and she was content to just enjoy the view. It was a beautiful March day, with only a few white puffy clouds to mar the blue sky.

Ryder flew over the vista point that drew so many tourists to Eagle's Ridge, taking her to a higher ridge farther to the east, with a view even more magnificent.

"Want to take a closer look?" Ryder asked.

She wasn't sure exactly what he meant, but she nodded. "Sure."

A minute later, she realized he was going to set the helicopter down on a patchy grass of land on top of a mountain.

"Whoa," she said. "Are you landing there?"

"Yes."

"It's so small," she protested.

"It's plenty big. Don't worry."

As the ground got closer, she realized the landing spot was larger than she'd first thought, and Ryder set the helicopter down with gentle ease. He pulled off his headset, urging her to do the same. "I want to show you one of my favorite views. Come on."

She jumped down to the ground, avoiding the still spinning blades, and followed Ryder over to the edge of the mountain they'd just landed on.

"What do you think?" he asked, sweeping his hand toward the view.

"It's magnificent. I feel like I'm on top of the world. It's much more impressive than the view from Eagle's Ridge, and I thought that was amazing." She stared out in awe at the Snake River winding its way through the valley below, the thick, tall trees, and sloping hills surrounding the city off in the distance. "This is crazy beautiful," she said, turning to Ryder. She couldn't read his eyes behind his aviator glasses, but she could see the smile crease his lips.

"It is," he agreed, taking off his glasses and tucking them into his shirt. "Which is why I wanted you to see it, Bailey. Because you're…you're crazy beautiful, too."

He pushed her sunglasses up on top of her head, smiled into her eyes, and then stole her breath with a hot, passionate kiss that made her feel like the world was spinning all around her, and the only anchor she had was him—his hands on her hips, his mouth on hers, his powerful body surrounding her like the Blue Mountains towering over them. She wrapped her arms around his neck, needing the best, most impulsive, reckless, and perfect kiss to go on as long as possible.

Ryder angled his mouth one way, then the other, his tongue sweeping inside, bringing even more heat, more desire. She felt like she'd just climbed onto a runaway train, intense feelings running through her that she hadn't even realized existed. She'd had relationships, boyfriends, but this—this felt really different and a little bit terrifying.

She couldn't let a man take over her world again. This was supposed to be her time to figure things out.

That thought finally gave her the strength to let go of Ryder. She stepped back. He stared at her with dark-blue eyes glittering with the passion they'd just shared.

"We can't do this," she said.

"I thought we did it pretty well. I'm waiting for the thunder and lightning."

She appreciated his attempt at humor because it gave her a chance to regroup. "I'd prefer to keep the sunshine. We do have to fly off this mountain at some point."

"We'll be fine, and this is your fault."

"Excuse me? How is it my fault?"

"It's your eyes. They're like the sky, the endlessly blue and ever-changing sky that pulls you in and doesn't let go. A man could get lost in that sky."

She took a quick breath at his words. She'd never had a man say something so poetic, so unexpected. "I—I don't know what to say."

"Don't say anything. Words will only ruin it."

She thought that was probably true, and when Ryder put his hands on her shoulders and turned her to face the view, she was happy to look out over the picturesque landscape, letting its restful beauty cool her heated emotions.

They stood there for several quiet minutes, her back against Ryder's solid chest. She couldn't bring herself to move away from his warmth, even though she knew she probably should. But that time would come soon enough. She'd ended the kiss. That was the important thing.

She just had to resist the urge to turn around and kiss him again, making a mockery of her very recent declaration that they could not do that.

"I first came here when I was about twenty-two," Ryder said, interrupting her thoughts. "It was right after I graduated from the Naval Academy. I had a few days off before I headed to flight school, so I came home for the weekend. David was actually at my house. He was visiting my grandfather. He told me he'd just gotten a new helicopter, and I should come by and try it out; so, I did. I wanted one last look at the valley before I left. I didn't know when I'd be back—it could be years—it could be never. So, I took the helo, and I ended up here."

She turned to face him. His gaze was now dark with shadows, and as he folded his arms in front of his chest and looked past her at the valley, she had the feeling he was very far away.

She felt a little foolish. She'd been thinking about their kiss, and he'd gone much further back in time. She wanted to know what he was thinking, why there was suddenly a sense of sadness about him. "Ryder?"

He started. "What?"

"Where did you go just now?"

He shrugged. "I don't know."

"You seemed sad all of a sudden."

"Just thinking."

"About what?"

"Random moments in life."

"Random or important? Maybe even life changing?" She could see that Ryder was holding something back, and she was more than a little curious about what it was.

"Those are deep questions," he said lightly.

"Well, we're standing on top of the world right now, so I think it's okay to be philosophical. In fact, this might be the best time for deep questions and less vague answers."

He gave her a faint smile. "It does feel like we're standing on top of the world, doesn't it?"

"To me it does. But you're a pilot. You fly even higher."

"It's different when you're on your feet."

"So, you said you came here before you went to flight school," she prodded. "What made you stop?"

"I was thinking about the past and about the future, wondering if I'd ever be back in the town that I loved but in some ways, I also hated."

"Really? You hated Eagle's Ridge? That surprises me. You were the best at everything."

"I was who people wanted me to be. Maybe that was the best, but it wasn't really who I was. That's why I left to go to the Naval Academy. My parents didn't want that for me. They wanted me to go to college in Washington or any other non-military institution."

She was surprised again. "But your family is part of the military tradition. Your mom often organizes fundraisers for the troops."

"Because it's the right thing to do, and she's very

big on her reputation."

"Well, I guess I can understand her not wanting you to serve. It's dangerous, and she was probably worried."

He shrugged off her answer as if it were the most ridiculous idea in the world.

"What? You don't think she worried about you?"

"No, I don't think she allowed herself to care that much."

"Ryder, that's crazy. Your mom loves you."

"You don't know anything about her."

"That might be true, but I can't believe she doesn't love you. She's so big on family and holidays and celebrations and you and your dad and your grandfather and aunts and uncles and cousins are always leading the way."

"All that is for show. It's for the town; it's what's expected. But when my parents are at home, away from the spotlight, it's a different story, especially at Christmas. The housekeeper puts up a tree and makes a meal, and we suffer through it together. We're all relieved when it's over."

Her brows drew together, perplexed by his words. "I don't get it. What am I missing?"

"Nothing. We don't need to talk about my family."

"Yes, we do. And you started it, so you have to finish. Why do you think your parents don't worry about you or don't love you?"

"Because they broke a long time ago—when Charlie died."

"Charlie?" she echoed, his words ringing a very distant bell.

He frowned. "You don't remember, do you? I

guess you wouldn't. You would have been a baby when it happened. Charlie was my older brother. He died when he was seven and I was five. We were in the park. His friend's puppy got off its leash, and Charlie went running after him. He was hit by a car. He died instantly."

Her stomach churned and her heart went out to him, the pain in his eyes as raw as it had probably been at the time. "I do remember hearing that story, but it was a long time ago. I'm sorry I forgot."

"You don't have to apologize; it was twenty-seven years ago, and frankly my parents stopped talking about Charlie long before the town did. In typical Westbrook fashion, they buried their feelings along with their son. After that, they shut down. I learned early on that asking about Charlie made my mother cry and my father disappear, so I stopped. Everything that belonged to Charlie vanished from the house. His bedroom was turned into a guestroom that no one ever went into."

"I'm surprised they didn't want to keep his memory alive."

"I wouldn't have handled it the way they did, but I can't fault them for dealing with their pain and grief in whatever way they chose to. Just like I can't really blame them for not knowing what to do with me."

"What do you mean? I would have thought that having lost Charlie, they'd be more than a little focused on you."

"I think it was just too hard to let love back in, especially for a child. All I knew back then was that I had to make up for him being gone. I had to be perfect. I had to be the leader, the athlete, the scholar—everything Charlie could have been if he'd lived. But the one thing Charlie wouldn't have done was go into the Navy. He'd get horrible motion sickness whenever we drove on a windy road or took a boat out on the river. Charlie preferred to keep his feet on solid ground."

"Is that what you remember most about him?"

"That and his laugh. It would come out like a burst of fireworks, no slow warm-up, just a big, deep series of belly laughs. It was contagious. I wouldn't even know what he was laughing at, but suddenly I was laughing, too." His lips curved at the memory. "I think he was a happy kid—at least, he is in my memories."

"I'm so sorry that he died."

"Me, too."

"Do your parents ever talk about him now?"

"Oh, no, never. I don't think Charlie's name has been mentioned since the funeral."

"I don't understand that."

"Westbrooks don't talk about feelings or really much of anything else. The silence in the house I grew up in could be deafening."

"That doesn't sound like a lot of fun."

"I wondered if it would have been different if Charlie hadn't died, but maybe it would have been the same. Who knows…"

Her heart swelled again for the lonely little boy Ryder must have been surrounded by cold parents, who were isolated from him by their grief. "I wish they'd done better by you. You should have had some support."

"To be fair, my parents could barely get through their own days. When I needed to escape, I took to the sky. When I flew, all my problems stayed behind.

Eventually, I knew that flying for the Navy was what I wanted to do."

"That makes sense, and after today's ride, I appreciate your passion even more."

He grinned. "My passion for flying or my passion for you?"

She made a face at him. "I have a feeling today's kiss was all tied up in a lot of other emotions. Being here is special for you."

"It is," he agreed. "But being here with you is even more special."

"Now I know how you got all the girls in high school; you really have a way with words, and with other things…"

The humorous glint in his eyes turned more serious. "I'm not trying to charm you, Bailey."

"You might not be trying, but you're still doing a pretty good job. You've learned more about me in the last few days than Franco did in six months."

"His loss."

"I haven't made the best decisions about men. I've let relationships derail my plans for myself. I don't want to do that anymore."

He nodded. "I get that. I've never let any relationship derail my plans, but now I'm starting to wonder if I spent so much time on the plans that I forgot to live."

"Is that why you came home? The unfinished business you mentioned last night?"

"Partly. It's probably a lost cause, but I feel like I spent my whole life waiting for my parents to open up to me, to let me in, to save me from the cold, but maybe I'm the one who needs to do that for them."

After what she'd just heard about his parents, she

was amazed he wanted to try.

"It probably won't work, and that's all right, but I have to give it a shot," he added. "At the end of the day, I want to be in Eagle's Ridge. It's home. And when you've been where I've been, home is a dream that not everyone gets to go back to. Plus, my grandfather is turning ninety-five years old on Tuesday. I don't know how much time he has left, and maybe it's too late for meaningful words—"

"But you have to give it a shot," she finished, repeating his earlier statement. "Are you sure you won't miss the Navy?"

"I'll miss the people, but I think I can do some good here."

"Running the airport?" she asked doubtfully. "That won't be too tame?"

"I'm going to fly, too—search and rescue, firefighting support, taking pretty blondes on sightseeing tours. It's all good."

Thinking about Ryder taking other women to what already felt like their special place didn't sound good to her at all, but she simply smiled and said, "Maybe we should get going. You still haven't shown me what land you want for the airport."

"I'll show you on the way back." He leaned in and stole a quick kiss. "In case you were wondering, what happens on the mountain stays on the mountain."

She was happy to hear that because she didn't think the Tuckers or the Westbrooks would be happy about anything that had just happened.

Nine

—➤➤➤◄◄◄◄←—

As Ryder flew back across the valley, he felt great, better than he had in a long time. It wasn't just the flight or the mountain view that had cleared his head; it was Bailey. He wasn't sure why he'd told her about Charlie; he certainly hadn't planned on bringing it up. But now that he had, it felt like a weight he hadn't even realized he was carrying had fallen off his shoulders.

He'd never been free to talk about Charlie in Eagle's Ridge, and when he was overseas, sharing that kind of information had been the furthest thing from his mind. But being on the mountain top, looking down at his life, his past, had taken him a long way back, and the words had poured out of him.

He'd told the truth when he'd said he wanted to make peace with his parents, but he'd been back in town for two months and he hadn't even gotten started on that endeavor. It wasn't easy to break through the solid wall between them. In fact, he'd barely seen either of his parents and now his grandfather was on his case about wanting to use Tucker land.

But he'd figure out his family later. Getting himself into a job he could love was his first priority and while he'd told Bailey he didn't want to spend his life making plans, he couldn't stop himself from focusing on the steps needed to turn the airport into a place he could expand and run with some sense of purpose. He certainly wasn't interested in just hanging around the airfield to welcome the passengers on the few puddle jumpers that showed up there. He needed more than that.

Which brought him back to the land that he needed.

"See the airfield?" he asked.

Bailey nodded.

"I want to expand the runway on the northern approach."

"I didn't even realize that was my grandfather's land. It's not near his house or the other family buildings."

"The land slopes up fairly quickly, but I only need the flat section that starts about a quarter-mile from the beginning of the current runway. I can't imagine there's any other use for it. It's right under the flight path, not very appealing for homes or other buildings."

"That's true. I wonder if he ever had a plan for it."

"I think it's more that he just can't bear to lose another inch of his land."

"Probably," she agreed. "Land is very important to him. We should go back now. I have to work at the diner tonight."

"You've got it."

After landing the helo a few minutes later, he walked Bailey out to her car, feeling an incredible reluctance to let her go. "Thanks for coming."

"I'm glad I did. The view was amazing. I can't believe I grew up here and never saw the town from that vantage point."

"Was it only the view that was amazing?" he said lightly.

"Fishing for compliments?"

"I like you, Bailey."

Surprise flashed across her face. "I like you, too."

"I sense there's a *but* coming... I hope it's not because I'm a Westbrook and you're a Tucker."

"Not really, although that won't make either of our families happy, but the real reason is that I don't know what I'm doing with my life, Ryder. Everything is up in the air, and I don't want to start something I can't finish."

Her words made a lot of sense, but they weren't ones he wanted to hear. "I get that, but I think we've already started, Bailey." He lowered his head and took another kiss, knowing he probably had only a split second before she got into her car and drove away.

Her lips were warm and sexy, and he wanted to linger. He wanted to take her home with him. But there was a part of him still able to hear warning bells, and that's what made him lift his head. She gave him an uncertain, somewhat yearning look, and he almost reached for her again.

But then she was opening her car door, and sliding behind the wheel, clearly determined to put some space between them. "Good-bye, Ryder."

"Not good-bye," he said firmly. "We still have a plan to execute."

"I'll talk to my grandfather tonight or tomorrow, but I can't promise I'll get you the answer you want."

"I understand." He shut the car door and stood back as she revved the engine and then pulled out of the lot.

He watched her drive away, feeling a sense of loss that shocked him. He didn't want her to leave Eagle's Ridge. He wanted them to have a chance to see what might happen between them. He'd left home to chase his dreams a long time ago, and he'd come back because he knew Eagle's Ridge was where he wanted to be. But Bailey still needed to figure out where she wanted to be and what she wanted to do. It wouldn't be fair or even smart to try to sway her. But he really wanted to...

So much for his single-minded focus on airport development.

Forcing himself to turn around, he headed back to the office.

After fifteen minutes of staring restlessly at his computer, completely unable to concentrate or think about anything but Bailey, he grabbed his keys and coat and walked out of his office.

While he was waiting for Bailey to talk to her grandfather, he would take another shot at the Westbrooks and the Founder's Day celebration. It was a long shot, but there was a slim chance he might get lucky.

Ryder entered his grandfather's house a little before five, surprised to hear laughter and voices in what was usually a very quiet household. In the living room, he found not only his mother but also his aunt, Catherine Garrison, and his great-aunt, Margaret

Garrison, who was his grandfather's younger sister. Catherine was married to Margaret's son Ben.

With his family was one of Eagle Ridge's most eccentric characters, the silver-haired Hildie Fontana, who ran Hildie's House, and was the main resource for anyone who wanted memorabilia or gossip.

"Is that Ryder?" Hildie asked, her unusually expressive eyebrows twitching as she gave him an appraising look. "I think you've gotten taller and even more handsome, if that's possible."

"And you've gotten even more beautiful," he returned.

Her eyes beamed with pleasure. "Well, it's good someone around here finally noticed," she said with a laugh.

His gaze swept the rest of the group, and he said hello to his aunt and great-aunt. There weren't any hugs exchanged—Westbrooks were not a hugging kind of family.

Catherine looked amazing as always, wearing tailored pants and a silky blouse, her dark-blonde hair pulled back in a bun. His mother matched her sister-in-law for style with a slim black skirt, high heels and a cardigan sweater. Margaret had also dressed for style in a dark-red knit dress and heels that made her look far younger than her eighty-eight years.

"So, what's going on around here?" he asked.

"Founders' Day weekend, of course," Hildie replied. "We're just finalizing our plans for Friday's more civic-minded events, with the parade and speeches from city leaders as well as the unveiling of a new John Westbrook statue in front of City Hall."

"Grandfather is getting another statue?" he asked in surprise. "Aren't there already three or four around town?"

"This one is being done by a renowned sculptor," his mother said. "The other ones really don't do John justice."

He decided not to argue her point, because he had more important battles to fight. "Okay. So, I'm glad you're all here. I wanted to make a suggestion about this weekend."

Four pairs of expectant eyes focused on him, wariness in their gazes.

He took a breath and jumped in. "What if we combine the Friday activities that are solely related to Grandfather and combine those with the weekend events? Make it one big weekend for all four founders, instead of two separate events. We can put an end to this ridiculous feud once and for all."

"I've told you before that won't work," his mother said quickly. "I don't know why you think it would, Ryder."

"Because it's time for the town to come together."

"This is about your runway again, isn't it?" his mother said with a long-suffering sigh. "It's not going to happen, Ryder. Your grandfather won't go for it, so it's a non-starter. You need to let it go."

"It's not just about a new runway; it's about bringing this town together. Aren't you all tired of having two sides to everything? If I could convince Grandfather, would the rest of you be willing to change up the events to include all the founders?"

"You'll never convince him," his mom said.

"But if I could…"

His mother gave a helpless shrug, looking at the others. "What do you all think?"

"I'd love to combine the events," Hildie said. "But

I think you'd be pulling off a miracle if you could make that happen, Ryder."

"I agree. I don't believe my brother will change his mind," Margaret put in. "He's ninety-five years old, and he's only changed his mind about three times in his entire life. I don't think we're going to get number four. He hates the Tuckers with every fiber of his being."

His gut tightened at that comment, a reminder that any relationship with Bailey was going to be complicated. He turned to his aunt. "What about you, Aunt Catherine?"

His aunt shrugged. "Honestly, it doesn't matter to me, Ryder. One weekend of events for everyone would be fine, but otherwise, I'm happy to do it the way we've always done it."

"Will Ford be coming into town?" he asked. If he could get his cousin on his side, that might help.

"I doubt it," his aunt said harshly. "He always has a million reasons why he can't come home."

"Nonsensical reasons," Margaret muttered. "That boy needs to own up to his responsibilities to this family."

"Getting back to our meeting," his mother interrupted. "I also wanted to talk about next Tuesday night—John's private birthday dinner."

"What's the plan for this year?" he asked.

"Your grandfather wants to stay home," his mother replied. "He won't admit it, but ever since he had that bad cold in the beginning of February, he's had a lot less energy. The weekend events will take a lot out of him, so we will have a catered family dinner. The problem is that we had Patrick Markham from Seattle lined up to fly in and cook for us, but he's under the weather, and now he can't make it. I'm worried that there's not enough time for us to get someone else to Eagle's Ridge."

"What about one of the restaurants here in town?" he asked. "Couldn't a local chef cater this dinner?"

"None of them are fancy enough," Margaret said. "It has to be special."

"I agree," his aunt interjected. "But I don't know what we're going to do. I already tried Victoria Hunt from Palermo's in Spokane. She said she's been booked for months and good luck trying to get anyone with this short of notice."

As the women continued to discuss their options, an idea took root in his head. They needed a chef and Bailey was one of the best. But if he put her name out, they'd immediately dismiss her out of hand. Maybe there was a way he could slide her in under the radar. If she cooked her fantastic food for his grandfather's birthday, it would be a good start to easing tension between the families and maybe…just maybe…he could talk to his grandfather about renting Veronica's to Bailey, give her a chance to have her own restaurant.

It was another long-shot idea. There seemed to be no shortage of them these days. And he didn't even know if Bailey's impulsive thought the night before was really something she wanted to do, but he'd sure love to give her a reason to consider staying in Eagle's Ridge, and this might be it. He'd seen the yearning in her eyes when she'd looked at the shuttered-up building the night before. She'd pictured a bustling restaurant with her at the helm, and he liked that picture.

"Why don't you let me take care of this?" he

suggested, his interruption bringing more questioning looks.

"You?" his mother echoed in surprise. "What are you going to do?"

"Make some calls. I know some chefs who might be interested."

"Like who?" she asked.

"Look, you're always telling me you want me to get more involved and help out," he said. "Let me do this. I promise you will not be disappointed. Dinner will be perfect."

The four women exchanged glances, then his mother finally said, "All right, I suppose so. But don't screw this up, Ryder. It's your grandfather's ninety-fifth birthday. It has to be great."

"It will be great. Don't worry another second about it. If you'll excuse me, I better get started making those calls." As he left the room, he let out a breath, wondering what on earth he'd just gotten himself into.

Now he just needed to convince Bailey to do him another favor…or he was going to have to find another chef and fast!

Ten

"You want me to do what?" Bailey asked in shock as Ryder confronted her when she was leaving the diner a little past eight o'clock that night.

She hadn't expected to see him again so soon. In fact, after she'd left the airport, she'd told herself that putting some distance between herself and Ryder would be a good idea.

It wasn't just kissing him on the mountain that had shaken her up; it was also how close she'd felt to him after he'd talked to her about his brother, shared a part of himself she had never known. Hearing about how he'd grown up with parents who'd shut down emotionally after the loss of their oldest son had touched her heart. No wonder Ryder had had to be perfect. He'd been trying to make up for so much and what a tremendous amount of pressure to always be under. But she couldn't let herself get so caught up in Ryder that she lost track of her own life.

But now that he was standing in front of her with a gleam of excitement in his eyes, after having laid out one of the worst plans she'd ever heard, she realized that Ryder was not going away any time soon, and she was both happy and worried about that.

"It's perfect," Ryder said. "You cook for my grandfather, and then I talk to him about letting the amazing chef, who dazzled him with her culinary genius, lease Veronica's and open a new restaurant. You could make it into whatever you want it to be."

"But—but even if he agreed, it still might be too expensive. I'd also need money to decorate and buy supplies—there's just so much that goes into opening a restaurant. How could I possibly do it?" She walked a few steps away from him and rested her hands on the rail overlooking the river. The water was swirling below, and it mirrored her emotions exactly.

"You could do it," Ryder said, coming up next to her. "I'll help you."

"You don't know anything about opening a restaurant."

He smiled and tipped his head. "Good point, but I know talent, drive, and determination when I see it, and you have all three."

"I cooked you one meal," she protested.

"It wasn't just that meal. I've heard how good you are."

"And how bad."

"Those were lies—we both know that. You can do this, Bailey. I know you can."

His belief in her was amazing, but she couldn't quite trust it. "You just want me to help you get your runway. You'll say anything to get me on your side, but I already told you I'd help you."

"Which is exactly why this has nothing to do with the runway," he said forcefully. "I saw your face last night when you looked at Veronica's. You were putting together your own restaurant in your head. You sat on the patio and looked out at the water and saw your future, didn't you?"

She drew in a breath and let it out. "Maybe I saw the possibility of a future. But your grandfather is not going to let me rent that building even if I make him an amazing birthday dinner. As soon as he finds out it's me, that will be the end of that."

"It's worth a shot, Bailey, and it's just one dinner to make. Why not take the chance?"

"You seem awfully invested in this," she commented.

"It's the perfect opportunity for you to shine and for us to take another step toward breaking down the feud between our families. Plus, you can't say no, because I already told my mother I'd find a chef for the birthday dinner."

"Who was going to do it?"

"Some chef from Seattle, who got sick."

"If I say no, you're in a mess of trouble."

He gave her the smile that made her stomach flutter. "Yes. Don't say no."

"How are you going to keep my identity a secret? I'll need to know what he likes and doesn't like—if he has any allergies, that kind of thing. And where am I going to cook the dinner? I'd rather do it at his house, if that's where the celebration is." Her gaze narrowed. "I thought you said you were the type of person who plans things out."

"Well, this time I acted spontaneously. The dinner will be at his house. There's a back entrance to the kitchen. I think I can keep everyone out except Leticia and the servers, and they won't care. It will work. If you say yes, I'll make it happen."

It was almost impossible to consider saying no to his request. He was so excited about his idea; it was just one dinner, and it wasn't like she was so busy she couldn't help him out. "Well, it would be kind of fun to dazzle your grandfather and your family with my cooking skills."

"Wouldn't it?"

"All right. I'll do it. But you're going to have to find out what kind of food your grandfather and your family is expecting."

"I'll do some reconnaissance work tomorrow. So, you're on board?"

"I'm on board," she said, startled again when he wrapped his arms around her in a happy hug.

She couldn't help but hug him back and when he lifted his head, she was the one who took it one step further, planting a long and needy kiss on his lips. She was starting to feel like she was addicted to his taste, to his touch, to everything about him.

"What the hell! Bailey?"

She broke away from Ryder at the sound of a familiar and shocked male voice and found herself staring straight into her brother Adam's blue eyes.

"You and…and Westbrook?" Adam said, as if he couldn't believe what he'd just witnessed. "What's going on?"

"We're…" She really couldn't come up with an explanation for what was going on, so she settled with one lame word. "Friends."

"A little more than that actually," Ryder put in.

She shot him a dark look. "That's not helpful."

"How long has this been going on?" Adam asked. "Is this why you came back, Bailey?"

"No. I came back because of a lot of reasons—

none of which have to do with Ryder."

"Wait. I get it," Adam said, hostility in his gaze as he looked at Ryder. "This is about you wanting to get Tucker land for the runway. Zane told me about your idea. You're using Bailey."

"I'm not using her," Ryder said sharply.

"He's not using me," she echoed, seeing the alpha side of both of them begin to take hold as they each straightened and stiffened and looked like they were ready to do battle. They might both be out of the service, but they were still warriors. "He's not," she repeated firmly, stepping between them and breaking the hard gaze they had going on. "Ryder has been completely up front about what he wants and I've agreed to help him get Grandpa to listen to his plans. The runway expansion would help your business, Adam. It would be great for the town."

"He knows all that," Ryder said with annoyance.

"I do know all that," Adam retorted. "What I still don't know is why you're messing around with my sister."

"I kissed him," she said.

"I thought you had a guy in New York," Adam said.

"Well, I don't. I'm single and free to kiss whoever I want, wherever I want."

"But he's a Westbrook."

"You and Zane are friends with him, aren't you?"

"More or less," Adam said, still giving Ryder a suspicious look.

"We are friends, and it's time this nonsensical feud ended," Ryder said.

"Ryder is right," she said. "And you know that, Adam."

"Maybe, but I still don't know if I like this." He waved his hand at the two of them, then turned his gaze on Ryder. "Bailey got hurt in New York. She won't tell us what happened, but we all know it was bad. I don't want her to get hurt again."

"Neither do I," Ryder said. "The last thing I want to do is hurt Bailey."

"Hey, I'm right here," she said. "And I make my own decisions. Right now, my decision is to leave. So, you two can do whatever you want to do—scowl at each other, throw down some punches, have a beer—I don't care. I'll see you both tomorrow."

She walked away, feeling as if she'd managed to regain a tiny bit of control over the situation, but when she reached the corner and took a quick glance over her shoulder, she couldn't help wondering what Adam and Ryder were talking about now.

———————

"Let's get a beer," Ryder suggested. "Baldie's?"

Adam hesitated, then said, "I was actually on my way over there to meet Zane."

"Perfect. I'll meet you there."

"All right."

Ryder walked back to his Jeep and started the engine, blowing out a tense breath as he did so. He hadn't anticipated Adam's negative reaction to seeing him kissing Bailey, but maybe he should have. The Tuckers were a tight family. And he didn't think it was just his name that was the problem; he doubted Adam would like anyone kissing his sister.

But he wasn't anyone, and he wasn't going to hurt Bailey. He needed Adam to understand that—Zane, too. The last thing he needed was more misunderstandings between the Tuckers and the Westbrooks.

A few minutes later, he pulled into the parking lot next to Baldie's, a local bar known for its impressive list of craft beers, classic rock jukebox, and the greasiest, most delicious cheese fries known to man.

Adam was already sliding into a chair across from Zane when Ryder walked in. Side-by-side, the Tucker brothers were impressive, although in childhood Zane had been known as the sickly, scrawny one. He'd suffered so many respiratory illnesses, he'd barely made it to school during the damp winter seasons, but somewhere along the way, Zane had found his health and had grown even taller and broader than his brother.

The twins were tight—always had been. Adam tended to be a bit more on the serious, intense side, while Zane was easygoing and always looking for a bet to make or to win. They'd all grown up playing sports together, but it really wasn't until he'd landed in detention the spring semester of his senior year that he'd really gotten to know them and to like them.

While they'd occasionally gotten together for drinks over the years, now that they were back in the same town, he was looking forward to a closer friendship.

But first he obviously had some peace to make...

"Looks like we'll take three Blue Mountain lagers," Zane told the waitress as he sat down. "Okay with you, Ryder?"

"Absolutely," he said.

A somewhat awkward silence fell between them after the waitress left.

Zane sent them both an inquisitive look. "Did I miss something? Or did you two bet on how long it would take before I start talking?"

"Ryder was kissing Bailey," Adam ground out, folding his arms across his chest.

Zane's brow shot up in surprise. "You were kissing my sister? When did that start?"

"When she got back," he said. "And for the record, she kissed me tonight."

"Tonight, huh?" Zane said. "Sounds like we're talking about more than one kiss."

"Look, all that matters is that I like Bailey, and she seems to like me," he replied. "That's it."

"No way is that it," Adam said. "She just got out of a relationship. And she came home to recover."

"Is that what she told you?" Zane asked his brother. "I thought it had something to do with people getting sick at her restaurant."

"Her boss—her boyfriend—threw her under the bus," Adam said, turning his attention to Zane. "At least, that's what everyone seems to think. She hasn't actually talked to me about it. Has she talked to you?"

"Not me," Zane replied. "She keeps saying she's busy or not ready to talk. Dad said let her be, so I've let her be. But maybe that was a mistake."

"We definitely need to talk to her," Adam agreed. "Especially now."

Ryder cleared his throat as both men looked back at him.

"What do you know, Ryder?" Zane asked. "Is Bailey talking to you?"

"She told me a little about what happened in New York," he admitted.

"Told *him*—not us," Zane pointed out to Adam.

"Yeah, I'm aware," Adam said grumpily.

Ryder was more than happy to see the waitress arrive with their beers. He lifted the bottle, took a long draught, and then said, "You two might not like the idea of me and Bailey together, but the only opinion I care about right now is hers. I appreciate that you worry about her, that she's your sister, but she's also a grown woman."

"With a last name your family hates," Adam reminded him.

"The three of us got past the feud back in high school, didn't we?" Ryder challenged. "Is this really going to be a problem?"

"It's only going to be a problem if you hurt her," Zane said pointedly.

"Then we'll have to kick your ass," Adam said.

"Otherwise...it's up to Bailey to decide what she wants," Zane added.

"Agreed," he said. "It's up to Bailey."

"I don't like your chances, Ryder," Zane continued. "If I were a betting man—"

"Which you are," he said dryly.

"I'd bet that Bailey goes back to New York and leaves you with a broken heart. This town is too small for her. She has always said that."

He took another sip of his beer. "I won't take that bet, but I will take the risk. And that's all I'm going to say on it right now. So, what else is going on? Anyone heard from Noah or Wyatt lately?" Both Noah and Wyatt were Navy SEALs, although they worked in very different parts of the world.

"Nothing," Adam said. "But they're often out of touch for weeks at a time."

"True," he said, reaching for the bowl of pretzels

on the table. "We should order some cheese fries."

"Good idea," Zane said, signaling for the waitress.

After ordering up three burgers and three cheese fries, one with a side of chili, he said, "I texted Jack about coming to Founders' Day weekend. Now that he's out of the service and living in Seattle, it's not a big trip. He said he'd try, but I'm not counting on it. There's something off with him."

"I agree," Zane said. "I hope he shows up this weekend. It would be good to catch up."

"It would," he said, sipping his beer. "By the way, Adam, if I can get my runway expansion through, I'm going to need some experienced search and rescue swimmers for that part of the business. I was thinking you might want to be a part of the crew."

An uneasy gleam passed through Adam's eyes. "I don't know. I'm busy with A To Z Watersports. I might not have the time. I've got a lot of plans I'm working on."

He was surprised Adam wasn't jumping on the suggestion. "Well, think about it. You don't have to decide right now. And it wouldn't be full-time, just when we really need you."

"I'll see," Adam said, taking a swig of his beer.

"I like your plans for the airport, Ryder," Zane put in. "But like I told you before, I don't think you're going to get Tucker land, so I hope you have an alternative in mind."

"There aren't any other alternatives without completely moving the airport, which is not anything the city wants to do, but Bailey said she'd talk to your grandfather for me. I'm hoping she'll have some pull."

"If anyone can work miracles with our

grandfather, it's Bailey," Zane said. "But I still wouldn't bet on it."

Which meant the odds were about as long as they could be, because Zane would bet on anything.

Eleven

Bailey worked alongside her father during Saturday morning's breakfast rush and then headed off to see her grandfather. She'd been putting that conversation off, but she needed to get to it, find out where her grandfather stood on the land issue and figure out if she had any chance of helping Ryder with his plans.

She walked back to her father's house, then hopped into the car and drove the two miles to her grandfather's home. The rain that had held off all morning suddenly broke as she got out of the vehicle. Fortunately, she'd grabbed an over-sized poncho from her father's closet before she left. Unfortunately, the strong wind and slanted rain burst soaked her in the short distance it took to walk from the car to the house.

"Bailey," Max Tucker said in surprise as he opened the door for her. "I didn't know you were coming out here today."

"I wanted to surprise you." She took off her poncho and hung it on a hook in the entry. Then she gave him a quick hug. "Sorry, I'm a little wet. It's pouring out there."

"Come and sit by the fire." He led her into the small living room, and she felt a wave of nostalgia at the sight of the blue sofa and matching loveseat, and the worn recliner next to the floor lamp where her grandfather spent most of his days. Above the fireplace was a television, framed on both sides by bookshelves filled with books. Her grandfather had always been a fan of war novels and thrillers, and judging by the ragged look of the books, he'd read many of them several times.

Max Tucker had lived in this two-bedroom house for as long as he'd been in Eagle's Ridge. He'd built it with his own hands, and he'd never wanted to live anywhere else. Even after his wife had died, he'd refused to leave. She could understand why. There were touches of her grandmother, Rebecca, everywhere, from the hand-sewn curtains over the windows, to the watercolor paintings of river and mountain life that she'd picked up at local art fairs, to the crocheted afghan on the back of the sofa.

She sat down on the brick bench in front of the fireplace as her grandfather took a seat in the recliner. His gray hair had thinned down to only a few strands and there were more lines on his weathered face, but at ninety-three years old, he looked damned good, and his blue eyes were very alert. She felt lucky every day to have had him in her life for so long. "How are you doing, Grandpa?"

"Well enough. I hear you've had some trouble."

"Yes, but I'm working my way out of it."

He gave her an approving nod. "That's what Tuckers do. When we get knocked down, we get right back up."

"I'm trying."

"It's good you came home. You should stay—take over No Man's Land, or work somewhere else if you want something fancy. People eat here just the same as they do in New York. I don't know why you can't cook here."

"I'm considering all my options. I know change can be a good thing," she added tentatively, slowly working her way toward where she needed to go. "Like when Dad moved the diner to the bridge. That was a good idea. Business doubled."

His gaze narrowed suspiciously. "Something on your mind, Bailey?"

She nervously licked her lips, not wanting to blow things apart before she had a chance to make her case. "Zane and Adam are working hard to build up their business and the restaurant can always use more customers. I know Eagle's Ridge is growing, but it could grow faster, if it was easier for tourists to get here."

Her grandfather didn't say a word, but there was a tension and a simmering anger in his gaze. "I've heard some rumors that Westbrook wants my land to extend the runway. Is that what you're talking about?"

"Yes. I think it might be something to consider. I'm sure you'd get a good price for it. And a larger airport would be good for everyone in Eagle's Ridge."

"Especially the Westbrooks," he ground out. "John took all of my good land, and now he wants more. There's no way in hell that's happening, not while I'm alive."

She swallowed hard at the harsh tone of his words. Her grandfather had always been loving and loyal to family and friends, but where the Westbrooks were concerned, he only saw red. "You wouldn't be selling the land to John Westbrook; you'd be selling it to Ryder and eventually to the city when they have enough money to buy Ryder out. In the long run, it's the whole town that benefits."

"No."

The harsh finality of his answer made it difficult to argue, but she couldn't just give up.

"What if you hear Ryder out, give him a chance to tell you exactly what he wants to do? There's a search and rescue aspect to the airfield operations that would also provide an important service to the city. This isn't about the Westbrooks."

"It is as long as a Westbrook is doing the buying."

"I don't understand. How can your anger toward one man be so strong after so many years? How can it color every decision you make? How can it stop you from doing something good for our own family just because someone else might benefit?" Her passion grew with her questions. It wasn't just Ryder she was fighting for; it was something more, something she couldn't really even define. But she was tired of being told no. "Our family is never going to use that strip of land. It's right under the flight path. It's just sitting there, when it could be doing some good."

His face had paled during her speech, his blue eyes dark with emotion. "You don't know what went on between Westbrook and me, Bailey."

"I know what you've always told me about the poker game, the drinking, the bad bet, but you've never really explained the part about Veronica. Were you in love with her?

He gazed into the fire for a moment and then looked back at her. "I did love Veronica. But like everyone else in this town, she fell for the Westbrook charm, and John stole her away from me."

"I know it's painful when someone you love chooses someone else," she said carefully. "But what about Grandma? Didn't you love her? Weren't you happy together? Didn't you end up with the true love of your life?"

"Of course, I did. Veronica has nothing to do with Rebecca."

"It seems to me that you and Grandma made a wonderful life for yourselves and for our family. So maybe things worked out the way they were meant to."

"You're not going to talk me into this land deal, Bailey."

"I'm not trying to. I just want you to agree to meet with Ryder. He's a good guy—a soldier, a Navy pilot—just like you. He's not his grandfather; he's his own man. Give him a chance to lay out his plan. Can you do that?"

"It sounds to me like you're sweet on him."

It was an old-fashioned way to describe the intense attraction she had to Ryder, but she certainly couldn't deny it. "I do like him."

"He's a Westbrook."

"I can't let his last name be the obstacle between us, Grandpa. I can't fight your fight. I don't want to be disloyal to our family, but Ryder isn't his grandfather, and I'm not you." She blew out a breath. "I'm not trying to hurt you. And if I didn't think Ryder's idea was a good one for our family, I wouldn't be here."

"You're a lot like your grandmother," he muttered.

She had a feeling her grandmother had not been a

big fan of the feud, either. "Does that mean you'll meet with Ryder?"

He chewed on his bottom lip while he pondered her question. Finally, he said, "You can bring him by tomorrow. If I'm going to listen to him, you are, too."

She was thrilled to have made it over the first hurdle. "Okay. How about around ten thirty? I'm helping Dad at the diner this week, so that's a good time between breakfast and lunch."

"I'll be here."

She got to her feet. "I should get back to work."

"I'll walk you out."

She put on her damp poncho as her grandfather opened the door. The rain had lessened to barely a drizzle. "Well, that was fast. I hope that's the worst of the storm. I couldn't help noticing how high the river is."

"It's been a wet winter. But it will be fine. I've lived by this river for more than six decades, and I know its moods. Right now, she's running high and fast, showing off her stuff, but in a few weeks, she will be back to peaceful and calm, ready to entertain the tourists."

"You make the river sound like a person, Grandpa."

"Sometimes she's a stubborn and contrary woman, much like someone else I know."

"I'm a Tucker," she said with a grin. "Stubbornness is in our DNA. I'll see you tomorrow. And be nice to Ryder."

"I know you won't listen to my advice, Bailey, but a Westbrook is always going to look out for himself first. I don't want that for you. You deserve better. So, you should ask yourself if it's really the expanded airport runway you want, or if it's Ryder. If it's him, think twice, or three times."

She didn't reply, just gave her grandfather a kiss on the cheek and said, "I'll see you tomorrow. And don't worry, I know what I'm doing."

At least, she hoped she did.

On her way back to the diner, Bailey pulled out her phone to call Ryder. Just the thought of hearing his voice immediately sent blood rushing through her veins. And when he did come on the line, her heart skipped a beat.

"Bailey," he said, a warm, husky note in his voice that told her he was happy to hear from her. "How are you?"

"I'm good. Are you at work? Am I interrupting?"

"I'm at work, but you're not interrupting. What's up?"

"I just spoke to my grandfather, and he's willing to hear you out."

"Are you serious? When?"

"Tomorrow morning, around ten thirty. Would that work?"

"I'll make it work. You really can work miracles with your grandfather."

"I wouldn't say that. He told me his answer is probably going to be no, but I did get him to agree to listen to your plan, so I hope you have a good presentation ready to go. It's still a long shot, Ryder."

"I'm just happy I get to take the shot."

"You can stop by the diner on the way over there tomorrow and pick me up. He wants me there, too."

"Even better. I would love to have you by my side."

And she wanted to be by his side—for far more than just a conversation with her grandfather.

"Bailey? Are you still there?" Ryder asked.

"Yes, I'm here," she said, putting a quick stop to a sexy daydream that kept running through her head.

"I want to see you tonight."

A shiver shot down her spine. She wanted to see him, too, but they were getting in too deep too fast. *Weren't they?*

"I—I don't think that's a good idea, Ryder," she forced herself to say. "We've seen each other every day this week."

"What's wrong with that?"

She searched for a good answer and couldn't come up with one.

Ryder jumped into the silence. "Why don't we meet up after work? I'll take you to dinner. We can talk about tomorrow. And we can also discuss my grandfather's birthday dinner."

Framing the evening in those terms made it easier to say yes.

"I guess that would work."

"And when we're not talking about our respective grandfathers, we can just enjoy being together. I want to see you, Bailey, and I think you want to see me."

"That might be true, but anything between you and me is complicated. Look at how Adam reacted when he caught us kissing last night."

"He's fine about it."

"Is he? What did he say to you after I left?" she asked, still curious about what had gone down between Ryder and her brothers.

"He said I better not hurt you. And Zane, of course, agreed with him."

"Zane?" she echoed. "When did you talk to Zane?"

"Adam and I went to Baldie's and had a beer with Zane."

She inwardly groaned. "So, Zane knows you kissed me, too?"

"He knows you kissed me," he corrected. "But does it really matter what your brothers think?"

"No," she admitted.

"Good. Why don't we have pizza tonight? We can go to Izzy's or I can pick it up, and we can eat at my place."

Being around other people would only get more people talking and wondering about them, but being alone with Ryder at his house seemed like trouble just waiting to happen.

Unfortunately, that kind of trouble was really appealing. "I'll meet you at your house at eight."

"Perfect. What do you like on your pizza?"

"Anything but pineapple."

"You got it. I'll see you soon, Bailey."

His promising words made her swallow hard. She told herself they were just going to talk, but she'd never been a very good liar—not even to herself.

Twelve

—➤➤❰❰◄—

Ryder made a stop at his grandfather's house on his way to the pizza parlor. He'd been thinking about Bailey all day, and he was thrilled she'd set up a meeting with her grandfather to help him get what he wanted. Now, he needed to help her. She wanted ideas about what his grandfather liked to eat. Since he didn't have a clue, he decided to ask the one person who could help him.

"Ryder, you're going to have to get your own key if you're going to visit this often," Leticia said, as she let him in the house.

"If anyone wanted me to have a key, they would have offered before now."

"Oh, I'm sure that's not true. Unfortunately, your parents are out, and your grandfather is napping."

"That's fine. I actually wanted to talk to you."

She closed the front door behind him. "What about?"

"Grandfather's birthday dinner on Tuesday night. I'm bringing in a chef."

"That's what your mother told me. I must admit I

was surprised. Who is it?"

He glanced around the marbled foyer, not wanting to have the conversation anywhere his grandfather might wander in. "Let's go into the kitchen."

"You sound secretive, but all right."

She led him down the hall and into the gourmet kitchen. As he glanced around the room, he thought Bailey would enjoy working here. Since they'd had many catered dinners over the years, the kitchen had all of the most modern equipment as well as a big selection of beautiful crystal glasses, china and silver.

"Would you like some coffee or tea?" Leticia asked.

"No, thanks."

"Then tell me who's going to be cooking in my kitchen."

While Leticia made the everyday meals for the family, she never cooked for parties or other events his parents or grandfather hosted. She'd said a long time ago that she didn't like the pressure, and she wasn't a fancy chef, but still he hoped he wasn't going to insult her in some way by bringing in Bailey. On the other hand, Bailey might be a better choice than some out-of-town chef, who would probably not treat Leticia that well.

"I will tell you, but first I have to ask you to make me a promise," he said. "I need to keep the identity of the chef a secret from everyone in the house until after the birthday dinner."

She gave him a speculative look. "And why on earth would I do that?"

"Because the person I have in mind is an amazing chef and will make a dinner to remember, if she's given the opportunity. But that won't happen if anyone finds out her last name."

Surprise moved through her gaze. "Are you talking about Bailey Tucker?"

"Yes. She's back in town, and she's a fantastic cook."

"I don't doubt that, but it's not a good idea, Ryder. This is your grandfather's ninety-fifth birthday. It's too important to risk having some big fight about the Tucker-Westbrook feud. Maybe another night..."

He understood her reservations, but he had to insist. "It has to be the birthday dinner."

"Why?"

"Because I want to end the feud, and it's the best time."

"How does Bailey cooking your grandfather's birthday dinner accomplish that?"

"He needs to realize that the Tuckers are not all bad, and that they have a lot to offer. Plus, Bailey is interested in leasing Veronica's and opening up her own restaurant there. I know Grandfather will dismiss the idea out of hand just because Bailey is a Tucker. I want to show him what she can do without him knowing it. Then I'll help her make the pitch."

She gave him a thoughtful look. "You're awfully worked up about this, Ryder. I don't think it's all about the feud, is it?"

"It's mostly about that."

"And the other part is that you're interested in Bailey—a pretty blonde with sky-blue eyes. You like her."

"I do," he admitted. "And she's the one woman my family will hate unless I can change their minds."

"Do you really care if they don't like her and you

do? You're your own man, Ryder; you always have
been. I think that's how you survived in a house that
got so cold after Charlie died."

He was almost shocked to hear Charlie's name
pass her lips.

"I know I'm not supposed to mention him,"
Leticia said. "But I also know how difficult things got
for you after he died, how hard you tried to make your
parents happy and proud. At some point, you realized
you couldn't fill that hole in their heart, and you
moved on with your life. I was happy when that
happened. Now I worry that you're back home and
you're getting caught up in old feuds that eventually
no one will remember."

"Thanks for recognizing how difficult things were
for me back then. But you don't have to worry. I know
what I want, and I'm going to do everything I can to
get it. Bailey has set up a meeting for me with her
grandfather about his land, and I want to give her a
shot at getting the restaurant. We're trading favors. All
I'm asking is that you don't tell anyone it's Bailey
doing the cooking."

"Even if I don't say anything, your mother will
come in to check on dinner and taste some of the food.
She likes to micromanage."

"I'm going to keep her out of the house that day. I
don't know how yet; but I'll figure something out."

"If you can do that, I'll keep my mouth shut."

"Thank you. Now, next question. Bailey wants to
cook my grandfather's favorite meal. Any ideas of
what he might like? She wants to make it really
special."

"Of course. I know exactly what he likes and
doesn't like. And if you really want to impress him, I

have the perfect idea. Come with me."

She moved across the kitchen and opened the door leading into the basement. He followed her down the stairs and across the well-organized storage room to a stack of plastic bins.

"It's in the top one," she said. "If you can get it down."

He grabbed the top bin off the stack and set it on a table. Pulling off the lid, he saw menus from Veronica's, as well as personal journals and loose recipe cards. "What's all this?"

"Your grandmother's recipes—some from the restaurant, some from elsewhere."

"But she didn't cook," he said in confusion.

"No, but she had her chefs whip up your grandfather's favorite meals. And every time they traveled somewhere and had an amazing lunch or dinner, she insisted on getting the recipe. She kept all of them in here and sometimes there are notes about the meal they had, where they were, what the occasion was. If Bailey wants to make your grandfather a meal to remember, then she should take him on a trip down memory lane."

"I was kind of hoping for just a few suggestions," he said, thinking the big bin was only going to put Bailey off.

"That might be easier, but it won't be as good. Let your Bailey decide if the items in this box inspire her or not."

He should say that she wasn't *his* Bailey, but he kind of liked the sound of that, so he simply put the lid back on the bin and said, "Okay, I'll do that. Thanks, Leticia."

"You're welcome. Do you think Bailey will stay

in town if she can open a restaurant here?"

"It might make a difference."

She gave him a knowing smile. "Then let's see if we can make that happen, because I'd like nothing more than for you to stay, too."

"My staying is not dependent on Bailey or anyone."

"No, but it's easier to stay home when home makes you really happy."

"We're not together," he forced himself to say. "You're jumping to conclusions."

"Maybe I am, and perhaps you and Bailey together is the worst possible idea, considering how much hatred there is between your families. On the other hand, the only way to end an old feud is probably through a great love story."

———※※※———

Leticia's words were still ringing through Ryder's head after he returned home. He put the pizza in the oven and then returned to the living room to make a fire. It was a cold and rainy night, but the house would be warm and inviting for Bailey.

Thinking about her brought him back to Leticia's suggestion that a great love story would end the feud.

He'd never really believed in once-in-a-lifetime love stories. He thought there were many different kinds of love stories one could have in life, but the big one, the one to triumph over all others…he wasn't so sure it existed.

He certainly hadn't seen evidence of that kind of passion in the house he'd grown up in. He supposed his parents loved each other, but they were rarely affectionate in front of him, and sometimes they didn't even seem like they liked each other all that much.

He knew they'd shut down after Charlie's death, and maybe in a way he had, too; he'd just been too young to realize it. Over the years, he'd had girlfriends, women he cared about—some he'd even considered having a relationship with—but there had always been other, more important goals in his life. Certainly, his military career had kept him busy and far, far away from home for years at a time. It had been easy to avoid anything deep and serious.

But his life was different now. He was in Eagle's Ridge. He was home. He couldn't use his normal list of excuses, and the truth was he didn't want to, at least not with Bailey. He wanted to see where things could go with her.

He hadn't felt such a sense of urgency in— forever.

But he felt it with her. He had to handle it carefully, because the last thing he wanted to do was scare her off. Unfortunately, going slow seemed like both the absolutely best idea and the absolutely worst idea he'd ever had.

Being with Bailey was both exhilarating and unsettling—emotions he liked a lot. Feeling nervous only meant something or someone was important. And he felt those nerves tighten now when bright headlights bounced off his front windows.

He grabbed the umbrella by the door and ran out to greet her. The rain had picked up again, and he didn't want her to get wet.

She got out of the car with a smile. "Thanks. I already got drenched once today."

"No problem." He held the umbrella over her

head as she grabbed her bag and closed the door. Then they ran across the drive to the porch. He opened the door for her, then shook out the umbrella and left it outside as he walked into the living room.

"It's nice in here. I like the fire," she said, as she took off her coat, revealing a pair of black jeans and a light-blue top that clung to her curves and accented her eyes.

God, she was pretty. How the hell was he going to keep his hands off her? His hands actually clenched in fists as he fought the desire running through his body. Tonight was supposed to be about pizza and planning, but the blood was rushing out of his head so fast, he could barely think.

"Ryder?" she said, an uncertain note in her voice. "You're staring."

"I can't help myself. You're beautiful, Bailey."

She licked her lips. "I was going to say how hungry I was and that I hope you got an extra-large pizza. But now…"

"Now?" His gut tightened as he saw the gleam of desire in her eyes.

"I'm hoping we can reheat it…later." She took a step forward, then paused.

"Don't." He shook his head at her hesitation. "Don't second-guess it."

He bridged the gap between them, framing her face with his hands. Her skin was soft and smooth, her hair silky. He'd always thought he had discipline, willpower, but Bailey's pink lips were just too damn inviting.

He brought his mouth down on hers with more force than he intended, but there was a hunger driving him that he hadn't felt before. He needed her, and he couldn't help but let her know it.

Bailey opened her mouth to his, and their tongues danced together in a tangle of passion, from which there would be no turning back.

When kissing her wasn't enough, he ran his mouth down the side of her jaw, his tongue tracing the curve of her ear, which brought forth a small moan of pleasure, and that only made him want to hear more. He slid his lips down her neck, wanting to taste every inch of her.

He raised his head, staring down at her bright wide gaze, her pink cheeks, her soft lips. "More." It wasn't a question but a statement.

"More," she agreed. "Much more."

He pulled a couple of condoms out of his pocket and tossed them on the coffee table.

"You're prepared," she murmured.

"Since I met you," he said with a smile.

"Do you know how crazy this is?"

"I'm thinking crazy good. What about you?"

She gave a helpless shrug. "I don't want to think anymore. I just want to feel." Moving forward, she grabbed the hem of his knit shirt. "This needs to come off."

"I agree." He helped her pull the shirt over his head, and then he tossed it on the ground.

He liked the way Bailey reached for him with greedy hands, her warm fingers drawing goose bumps along his skin as she caressed his abs. His body hardened in anticipation. He wanted everything to go faster, but he also didn't want to rush it.

Putting his hand around the nape of her neck, he pulled her toward him, going in for another kiss that went long and deep. Then he helped her off with her sweater, which quickly joined his shirt on the ground.

Her rose-colored bra was lacy, barely covering her full breasts. He flicked the bra open and pushed the straps off her shoulders as his hands covered her breasts, his thumbs playing with her nipples. She let out another sexy gasp as his mouth followed the path his hands had just taken.

And still it wasn't enough.

"Jeans," she ordered, her fingers reaching for the top button of his jeans.

His pulse raced even faster—if that was possible.

He kicked off his jeans and boxers, taking only a second to enjoy the look of female appreciation she gave him and the soft words, she uttered—"Oh, my,"—before helping her out of her own jeans, taking a silky thong down at the same time.

Bailey was a beautiful woman, everything he'd imagined and more. "Perfect," he whispered, gazing into her eyes. "You. This. Us."

She gave him a sexy smile. "I hope so. Let's find out."

As they fell down together on the sofa cushions, he proceeded to show her just how perfect they could be.

Thirteen

———⇒⇒⇒⇐⇐———

She hadn't felt this good in…she couldn't remember when. Bailey snuggled back against Ryder's broad, masculine chest as she gazed sleepily at the fire, a blaze that didn't begin to compare to the heat she and Ryder had just generated.

His arm tightened around her waist, and as he nuzzled her neck with his sexy mouth, she smiled in pure pleasure. Then she turned on her side, putting her arm around him as they faced each other.

"Well, did I say perfect or what?" he asked.

"It was perfect," she agreed. "I think you like a challenge."

"I think I like you," he said, brushing her lips with his.

"I like you, too." The words didn't really equate to the depth of emotion running through her. She didn't know how she'd fallen so hard and so fast, but she couldn't deny that Ryder had turned her life upside down. She'd come to Eagle's Ridge to lick her wounds, to figure out her life. She hadn't expected to fall for anyone—certainly not anyone with the last name of Westbrook.

Now what?

The question ran around in her head, but she didn't have an answer.

Maybe that was okay. Maybe she didn't need an answer. Maybe she just needed him.

"We should do all that again," she suggested. "In fact, I have a few other ideas."

"So do I. Should we go into the bedroom?"

"The fire is nice. And I feel…lazy."

"Me, too." His hand came to rest on her hip, his warm fingers teasing the laziness right out of her.

"Then you better stop that, or we'll be using a lot more energy really soon."

"I'm ready," he said with an enthusiasm that made her smile.

She threw her leg over his and planted her lips on his mouth and decided she was ready, too.

--->>><<<<--

It was after ten when they finally made it off the couch. After using the bathroom, she grabbed one of Ryder's T-shirts out of his drawer and wandered back into the kitchen.

Ryder had put on his jeans and was heating up the pizza in the oven. "It takes longer, but it's better than the microwave," he said.

"I agree."

"I like my shirt even better on you."

"I probably should have asked first."

"You never have to ask," he returned.

She sat down at the kitchen table and looked at a large plastic bin that was filled with papers and notebooks. "What's all this?"

"My grandmother's recipes and food journals, memories of her and my grandfather sharing trips and special meals," he replied. "Leticia gave it to me. She's my grandfather's housekeeper. She's been with him for about forty years, so she knows him as well as anyone does." He walked over to the table and popped open the lid on the bin. "I asked her to help you figure out the perfect meal for his birthday party, and she said you'd find the answer here."

"You told Leticia I agreed to cook dinner? What did she say?"

"That she thought it was a dangerous idea, but if I could keep my mother out of the kitchen, she wouldn't say anything."

"Maybe it is too dangerous, Ryder. I don't want to ruin your grandfather's ninety-fifth birthday party. It's such a special occasion."

"And you're an excellent chef. I know you can make an amazing meal."

"I know I can, too, but that won't matter when he finds out it's me cooking."

"He won't find out."

"Someone in your family will tell him. How will you keep your mother out of the kitchen?"

"Let me worry about that. All you have to do is agree to cook."

She picked up a menu from Veronica's restaurant and read through the entrees, which included quite a few classical French dishes: coquilles Saint-Jacques, which were scallops poached in white wine and placed atop a purée of mushrooms in a scallop shell, then gratinéed under a broiler; hachis Parmentier, the French version of shepherd's pie with a layer of mashed potatoes over beef; and a chocolate soufflé.

"I forgot that Veronica's served a lot of French dishes," she commented.

"My grandparents loved Paris. They went there on their honeymoon, and several times after that." Ryder returned to the oven, pulled out the pizza, and then grabbed plates out of the cupboard. "How many pieces do you want?"

"I'll start with two."

He brought over a plate with two slices of vegetable-laden pizza. "What would you like to drink?"

"Water is fine."

She picked up a slice of pizza and took a bite while she looked through some of the other items in the bin. Along with the menus, there were handwritten recipe cards, magazine recipes ripped out from wherever they'd first been printed, and several paper menus. One was from a café in Paris. She set down her pizza to take a better look. There was a handwritten note on the back of the menu.

Last night of our honeymoon. A rare blue moon, a walk along the Seine, a perfect meal with the most perfect chocolate soufflé.

"This is sweet," she said, handing the menu to Ryder, as he handed her a water bottle and set down a bowl of salad and a couple of forks.

"She sounds happy," he said.

"Very." She dug a little deeper and pulled out a photograph of a very young John and Veronica Westbrook. She suspected it had been taken on that same honeymoon trip. She flipped it over and read the short note aloud. "My beautiful bride. I never knew love could be like this. How lucky am I?" Pausing, she looked across the table at Ryder. "Your grandfather wrote this. I've always thought of him as a hard, angry man, but he obviously had another side. He loved your grandmother a lot."

"He's a complex man, and he has strong opinions on everything. There's no middle ground with him. And when he wants something, he gets it."

"Now that sounds more like the man my grandfather hates." She looked back at the bin, starting to get excited about making dinner for the Westbrooks. "I know what to do, Ryder. I'm going to bring back your grandfather's memories of Paris and Veronica and French cooking, which is what I love to cook anyway. You know, I spent a year in Paris learning how to cook French cuisine."

"I didn't know that. What a great experience. When did you do that?"

"Six years ago. It was a dream come true. I had just gotten out of culinary school in New York, and one of my instructors was going back to Paris to open a restaurant and he gave me a job. I started off at the bottom, making salads, and then graduated to sauces. Eventually, I was able to make some of the main dishes."

"Why did you leave?"

"He sold the restaurant to a new owner, who wanted to hire their own staff. I was very sad about it. After that, I traveled for two months through Italy and Spain, learning all I could about those cuisines, and then I headed to New York, hoping to put all my new skills to use. Unfortunately, it wasn't that easy to get just the right job. I worked at a couple of different places, some fairly mediocre. I was working at a French restaurant when Franco came in one night and decided to make me a job offer. At the time, I thought I was incredibly lucky, but it turned out my luck was all bad."

"I know it's easier to say let it go than to actually do it, but you have to try, Bailey. You can't change the decisions you made. You can't go back in time. And that's okay. Because, good or bad, our experiences make us who we are."

"That sounds very Zen," she said lightly. "Like something my yoga teacher would say."

He smiled. "I've never taken yoga, but I have learned that accepting reality and moving on is better than wasting time wishing things were different. You have a long life ahead of you and many more dreams to go after."

"Dreams that will be mine and not someone else's," she agreed. "I don't want to be second-in-command. I want to run my own restaurant. It's so clear to me now."

"And you'll do that. Maybe at Veronica's."

"It is in a great location, but we both know your grandfather will be tough to convince."

"We'll start with his birthday dinner and go from there."

"Can I take this bin home and look through it? I already have some ideas but I want to think about it."

"Of course. You can take it when you leave—in the morning."

A warm current ran through her at his words, and as she met his dark gaze, her heart skipped another beat. "You want me to spend the night?"

"I do. Very much. What about you?"

"Yes. And I think the rest of tonight should start right now." She grabbed his hand and pulled him to his feet.

"Wait! Have you had enough to eat?" he asked.

"Yes. What I haven't had enough of is you."

He took a quick breath. "You're going to kill me when you say things like that, Bailey."

"I don't plan on just using my words tonight," she said, pressing her hands against his bare chest as she moved on to her tiptoes to kiss him. "I have a lot of other things in mind."

"Show me," he said huskily, as he took her into the bedroom.

"You're late," her dad said, as Bailey rushed into the diner at seven thirty on Sunday morning. "And you didn't come home last night." He leaned against the kitchen counter and gave her a stern look. "I know you're a grown woman, but I still worry about you."

"I'm sorry." She hung up her coat, trying not to feel like a guilty teenager who'd missed curfew. But that was difficult to do, considering she'd recently jumped out of Ryder's bed, taken a quick shower and air-dried her hair on the way back to the diner. It was now curling in a riotous and revealing mess. "I should have let you know I wasn't coming home."

"Just tell me one thing. Are you all right?"

"I am," she replied, pulling her hair back into a ponytail.

He looked like he wanted to say something else, but in the end, he moved back toward the stove. "Then get to work. Sunday breakfast is our busiest meal of the day."

She was happy he hadn't asked where she'd spent

the night or who she was with, but then her dad had never been one to pry too deeply into her life. *Girl stuff,* as he called it, always made him uncomfortable.

She put on an apron and went to work. The next few hours flew by, and before she knew it, Brenda came in to tell her that Ryder was looking for her.

"I'll be right there," she said, finishing up an omelet.

"What are you doing with Westbrook?" her dad asked, as he flipped a batch of pancakes onto a plate and set it on the pass.

"I'm taking him to see Grandpa. He agreed to hear Ryder's plans for the airport."

Her father raised a disbelieving eyebrow. "Since when?"

"Since I spoke to him yesterday."

"Seriously?"

She nodded. "Yes."

"I can't believe he's going to let a Westbrook into his house."

"He told me to bring Ryder there."

Her dad shook his head in bemusement. "That's going to be a first."

"I hope it's the first step to a new relationship between our families. I don't want to be at war with the Westbrooks."

His sharp gaze swept over her once more. "I hope you know what you're doing, Bailey, and I'm not just talking about taking Ryder to see your grandfather."

"I know. I hope so, too." She grabbed her coat and bag and made her way out to the dining room.

Ryder was standing by the counter, chatting with Brenda, but when he saw her, his eyes flashed with welcome and remembered intimacy. Heat warmed her cheeks, revealing far too much when Brenda turned an inquiring gaze in her direction.

"Where are you two off to?" Brenda asked.

"To see Grandpa," she said.

Her words brought forth another shocked reaction. "You're going with Ryder to Max's house?"

"Yes."

"Then it must be a cold day in hell," Brenda said dryly.

"Ryder is not the devil," she said. "And it's about time my grandfather realized that."

She took Ryder's hand in hers, and walked out of the diner with him, knowing that everyone was watching them. Whatever their relationship was—it was definitely not a secret.

Fourteen

———⇒⇒❯❮⇐⇐←—

Ryder started the car and drove away from the restaurant, then surprised her by pulling over at the next street.

"Why are we stopping?" she asked.

"I haven't had a chance to kiss you yet."

As he leaned across the console, she met him halfway. The touch of his lips on hers took her back to the night before when they'd made sweet and sexy love for most of the night. Her memories made parts of her body ache with remembered pleasure and renewed desire. She could get addicted to Ryder. He knew just how to kiss her, touch her, taste her…drive her crazy.

He lifted his head and said, "That's better." Then he gave her such a sexy smile that her heart fluttered in her chest.

She'd sworn she was off men, but this man had pushed past all her resolutions, all her barriers. She'd let him in, and there was a part of her that was terrified that she'd made herself vulnerable, that she could get hurt again. But it was too late to go backward. And she couldn't bring herself to have any regrets, because Ryder made her feel so damn good about herself. If it ended, it ended; but right now, she was going to enjoy being with him.

"I do feel better," she admitted, meeting his gaze. "But we should go. Grandpa doesn't like it when people are late."

"Okay." He put the car back into drive and pulled out onto the road. They drove past her dad's house, and the meadow where Gambler had first wandered off and brought them together. She smiled to herself at the memory. Zane's neurotic dog and a bunch of frogs had certainly made their first meeting memorable.

When Ryder parked in front of her grandfather's house, she couldn't help noticing how high the river had risen since yesterday, lapping at the edge of the road in places, and there was more rain in the forecast for tonight and tomorrow.

"If the river gets much higher, this road is going to be underwater," she said, as they got out of the car.

"Your grandfather might want to stay at your dad's house for a couple of days."

She frowned, predicting that would not be an easy sell. "Maybe it won't get much worse."

"I hope not."

She could see that Ryder was distracted and not even looking at the water; his gaze was on the house. He was mentally prepping for his meeting with her grandfather, and she probably should be focusing on that as well.

"Just make him understand that the runway expansion is for the whole town, especially benefiting the Tucker family," she reminded him.

"I know what to say; I just hope he's ready to

listen."

"He's as ready as he's ever going to be."

She led the way up to the front door and rang the bell. Her grandfather answered a moment later, his expression about as cold and stubborn as she'd ever seen it, especially when his gaze landed on Ryder.

"Hello, Grandpa. This is Ryder Westbrook. And this is my grandfather, Max Tucker," she added, as the two men stared at each other.

The dislike in her grandfather's eyes bothered her. Ryder was becoming very important to her, and deep down she wanted to find a way for the two of them to like each other. That was probably a foolish hope.

When no one spoke, she said, "Can we come in, Grandpa?"

Max stepped back and waved them inside.

She wanted to slip her hand into Ryder's, but she didn't think that action would make this moment any easier and would probably only add an unnecessary complication by linking them together in a personal way. Instead, she sat down on the loveseat while Ryder took a seat on the couch and her grandfather opted for his recliner. A low fire burned in the fireplace, but there was a definite chill in the air.

"Thank you for seeing me, sir," Ryder began.

"Say what you have to say and then go," her grandfather returned.

She wanted to tell her grandfather to be nice, but she also sensed that it was her time to take a backseat and just listen.

Ryder presented his case in clear, concise, enthusiastic terms, the passion for his project evident in his voice as he spoke about economic benefits, making Eagle's Ridge an even better and bigger tourist destination, thereby helping Adam and Zane and all the other young men and women coming home from college or the service who wanted to make Eagle's Ridge their home but also needed to make money. In addition, he brought up the opportunity for better search and rescue operations for stranded hikers and injured rafters, and the wildfire abatement that could be started at the first sign of smoke.

Ryder was intelligent, charming, persuasive, and so good-looking, she thought, unable to take her gaze away from his strong profile, his handsome body, his intense words. When Ryder went all in on something, he was total commitment. He'd come today to make his case, and she couldn't imagine how her grandfather could say no to such a convincing argument.

She also couldn't imagine how she could ever say no to Ryder if he wanted her with the same conviction. No wonder he'd won everything in high school. No wonder he'd been the golden boy of Eagle's Ridge; he had a magnetism, a charisma, a way to connect with people that was truly impressive. And she knew it wasn't fake; he believed everything he was saying. Ryder was a warrior. He knew how to fight.

Unfortunately, her grandfather was a warrior, too, and he remained silent throughout, showing absolutely no reaction in his eyes. But he was listening to every word, which gave Bailey a small gleam of hope.

"The city would like to buy the land and eventually they will do that," Ryder finished. "But they don't have the budget now, so they need an intermediary. I know my last name isn't what you would want to see on a real-estate purchase, but this really isn't about me. I hope I've made that clear."

"Of course, it's about you," Max said, speaking for the first time. "It's what you want to do with your life, and you can't do it without the land."

"The land doesn't benefit you in any way," Ryder reminded him. "It's right under the flight path. You can't build homes there. It's no good for farming. It's only of value to the airport."

"But it's mine. It's what I have left—worthless, no-good land that your grandfather was happy to stick me with. Now you want it."

"If you got stuck with the land, then my offer should make you happy. This isn't charity. This is a business deal. You'll make money for something you consider worthless, and my grandfather has nothing to do with this. He didn't even want me to ask you."

"Because he knew I'd say no."

"Maybe you should surprise him and say yes," Ryder retorted.

Max stiffened in his chair and while Bailey couldn't be positive, she thought she saw a small hint of admiration in his eyes. Max Tucker liked strong people and Ryder was more than holding his own.

"Wouldn't you like to take some Westbrook money for land you can't use?" Ryder added. "What's the downside?"

"The Westbrooks win again by getting what they want."

"We all win, Grandpa," she put in. "All of us. That's the important thing."

"I—I don't know," Max said, a scowl on his face.

She was shocked that he didn't know. While she'd tried to be positive and hopeful, she'd really thought in the end her grandfather would just give Ryder a flat-out *no*.

"Will you think about it?" Ryder asked. "Talk to David about it. He's in favor of the idea."

Her grandfather's dark stare had her heart racing, but Ryder wasn't at all intimidated.

Finally, her grandfather blew out a breath and stood up. "I'll think on it. You two can go now."

"Thank you for hearing me out, sir," Ryder said.

As they stood up and followed her grandfather to the door, she brought up the other issue on her mind. "Grandpa, I'm worried about the river. It's awfully high. What if it comes over the road? You'll be stranded. Why don't you move to Dad's house for a few days? We're on higher ground there, no danger of flooding."

He immediately shook his head. "I'll be fine here."

"There's more rain coming."

"I have a generator and plenty of food and water. I can stay off the road for a few days if I have to. You don't need to worry."

She frowned. "I'm going to keep checking on you."

"Well, I can't stop you from doing that," he said, a small smile coming into his eyes when he looked at her.

She kissed him on the cheek, then hung back as Ryder moved toward the car. "Ryder is a good man. Does it really matter what his last name his?"

"It always has," he said, his smile fading.

"Then maybe it's time to change that."

"I'm too old to change."

"Or maybe you're just old enough," she

countered. "I'll see you later. Be safe."

"I will."

She walked down the steps, and got into Ryder's car. He started the engine without a word and drove down the road.

She was a little surprised by his silence. "What are you thinking?" she asked. "I thought that went better than I was expecting."

"Really?" He gave her a sharp look. "I don't think your grandfather is going to sell me that land."

The earlier determination in his gaze had changed to anger and frustration.

"He said he'd think about it. That wasn't a no; that was a maybe," she said.

"He just didn't want to say no in front of you."

"He's never had a problem with that before," she said dryly.

"Where am I taking you, Bailey? Home? Back to the diner? Where do you want to go?"

She kind of wished he'd included his house on the list. All traces of the man who couldn't wait to kiss her had vanished. He was a million miles away in his head. "The diner is good."

"Okay."

They didn't speak the rest of the way there. When he pulled into a parking spot in front of the restaurant, he didn't bother to turn off the engine.

She glanced over at him, not liking the way things were ending. She felt a coldness between them that seemed at odds with all the heat they'd made the night before. "Are you all right, Ryder?"

"I'm fine. Thanks for doing that with me."

"You don't seem fine."

He shrugged. "It is what it is, Bailey."

"I'm sorry he didn't say yes. But I still think there's a shot."

"You're dreaming. There's no shot. There's no runway. It's not happening. Your grandfather is going to carry on this feud for the rest of his life." Anger lit up his voice.

"I think you made some inroads with him today," she said. "You were very persuasive."

"I could have talked until I was blue in the face. He already has his mind made up."

She wanted to say that wasn't true, but maybe it was. Still… "So, what?" she challenged. "You're going to quit?"

"I didn't say that," he muttered.

"It sounded like it."

"I need to think, Bailey. You should go to work."

"All right, but call me if you want to do some thinking together."

"I'll do that."

She didn't believe him, but there was nothing to do but get out of the car. She shut the door and watched him drive away, frustrated that he'd shut her down and pushed her away when she'd been doing all she could to help him. She knew his anger was really at her grandfather, but she couldn't help but feel she was now a part of that anger. Maybe their last names were going to be too big of an obstacle between them.

She didn't want to think that Ryder had been using her to get to her grandfather and now he was done. But his brush-off had definitely stung.

Sighing, she couldn't help thinking that her life would be a lot simpler without so many stubborn, strong, prideful men in it.

He was an idiot. *What the hell was wrong with him?* He'd just taken out his frustration and anger on Bailey, when she'd gone out of her way to help him.

Ryder slammed on the brakes at the next stop and made a quick U-turn. No matter what her grandfather decided, he wanted Bailey in his life. And he needed her to know that. Last night had been quite possibly the best night of his life. He might not be able to get the land he wanted, but he wasn't going to lose her— certainly not because of her stubborn, feud-obsessed grandfather.

Although, he hadn't done himself any favors by behaving like an ass. He needed to fix that.

He pulled back into the parking spot he'd just left and walked into the diner.

Bailey was sitting at the counter, drinking coffee and chatting with Brenda. He was relieved she wasn't already at work in the kitchen.

Wary surprise flashed through her blue eyes when he walked up to her. "I thought you left."

He heard the unhappy, irritated note in her voice. "I'm sorry."

"You should be. You acted like a jerk, Ryder. I was trying to help you."

He tipped his head. "I know. Can you forgive me?"

"I'll have to think about it," she said, but there was a light in her eyes that told him he was at least halfway back to being in her good graces, and he felt a shockingly big amount of relief about that. There was a part of him that wondered how he'd let this woman come to mean so much to him so fast, and maybe he should slow down. On the other hand, life was short, and he didn't want to waste any more minutes of it.

"While Bailey is thinking about your apology, do you want some lunch?" Brenda asked with a gleam in her eyes. "Sam is whipping up a cheeseburger for his daughter; I'm sure he'd make you one, too."

"I will," Sam said, sticking his head through the window pass leading into the kitchen. "How do you like your burger, Ryder?"

"Medium is great," he said, sliding into the counter stool next to Bailey.

"Too bad we don't serve alcohol here," Sam added with a knowing smile. "I bet you could use a beer after talking to my dad."

"If you were pouring, I'd definitely say yes," he conceded, glad that neither Brenda nor Sam seemed upset with him. Maybe Bailey hadn't told them how he'd practically kicked her out of the car.

"Bailey says things went a little better than expected," Brenda said.

"I'll go with her take on it." Maybe he should be more optimistic that Max hadn't given him an outright no, but he still felt like he was a long way from yes.

A cool breeze came into the dining room as the door opened. Bailey turned her head and let out a gasp. He followed her gaze to a tall, dark-haired, dark-eyed man with olive skin.

The man wore black slacks and a button-down shirt under a black wool coat. In one hand was a huge bouquet of flowers and in the other was a magazine. He stopped three feet away from them, his gaze fixed on Bailey.

Ryder felt a pit grow in his stomach. He knew who this was even though Bailey hadn't said a word.

She seemed speechless, and he didn't like that at all.

"My love," the man said with a dramatic flair.

"What are you doing here, Franco?" Bailey asked, sliding off her chair to stand and face him.

"I have come to offer my deepest apologies. I am very sorry that I hurt you, Bailey. I have come to get you back. I will do anything to make that happen."

"It's too late," she said.

"It's not." Franco held up the magazine in his other hand. "I've told the world of my mistakes, that you are the finest chef, and that nothing that happened in the restaurant was your fault. They have printed a correction to the previous story. So, I have fixed everything. You will come back and run the restaurant. I will give you free rein to do whatever you want."

"You actually told the truth?" Bailey asked in disbelief.

"Yes. Because I love you, and I need you."

Ryder held his breath, waiting for Bailey to tell Franco she was done with him. She wasn't coming back. She wasn't his love. She didn't want anything from him. But Bailey seemed to be having trouble forming words.

Renewed anger rushed through him in a crushing wave. He'd come back to apologize to Bailey so that she would know how much she meant to him. But seeing her now with this guy made him wonder why the hell he'd bothered.

Bailey obviously still had feelings for the man, or she would have kicked him to the curb the first second he opened his mouth.

How could he have misread her so badly? He'd thought she was on the same page as him when she obviously wasn't.

Shooting out of his stool, he brushed past Franco, almost knocking the damn bouquet out of his hands.

"Wait, Ryder!" Bailey said.

He slammed the door to the diner on her plea and got into his Jeep. He caught a glimpse of her coming out of the restaurant as he took off down the street. He didn't need to hear anything from her. Words didn't matter. The silence he'd just witnessed had told him everything he needed to know.

⇌⊷⊶⇋

Bailey couldn't believe Ryder had just left in a storm of anger, without giving her a chance to say anything to him or to Franco. Nor could she believe Franco had just come back with apologies and retractions, something she'd never expected to happen.

She turned around as Franco came out of the restaurant. He must have left the flowers and magazine on the counter, because he was now empty-handed.

"Bailey," he said with concern. "What's going on? Who was that man?"

"Why are you really here?" she asked, ignoring his questions.

"I told you. I want you back—in my life and in my restaurant. I'm sorry for the misunderstanding. I was distraught after opening night. I wasn't speaking clearly. I didn't mean to throw the blame on you."

"Yes, you did," she said flatly. "You might be sorry now, but you lied to save yourself, and you threw me under the bus."

"It was a difficult time."

"Yes, it was—for me, too, but you left me to hang. You ruined my reputation. I can't forgive you for that."

"I will make it up to you. I will give you whatever you want—any restaurant of your choosing," he said. "If you want Paris, it's yours. London? It's yours. I need you, Bailey."

"Why?" she asked in confusion. "Why would you need me?"

"Because you're incredibly good, the best chef I've ever worked with."

She couldn't help feeling somewhat mollified by his words but not enough to forget everything that had happened. "I am a good chef, Franco. And I'll be even better without you holding me back. After you fired me, after I found out how little our relationship meant to you, I was hurt, angry. I ran away. But since I came home, I realized that I don't need you to be successful or happy. I never did. Everything I want I can get for myself, and I intend to do just that. We're done."

"You don't mean that. I can open doors for you."

"I can open my own doors. Maybe it will take longer. But I'll get where I need to go. Don't call me again. Don't come back here. I'm moving on with my life, and there is no place in it for you."

"Bailey, you can't mean this," he pleaded, shock in his eyes at her response. "You have to give me a chance. I've publicly apologized. The press is waiting for your return. I've already planned a new opening night."

Now she knew why he'd come back. Her return would provide more interest for that opening. "You'll have to open without me. I wish you well, Franco. I learned a lot from you."

"You've changed," he said, confusion in his gaze.

"I have," she agreed. "I've changed back into the woman I used to be, and I like her a lot better than the woman I was with you in New York. Goodbye, Franco." And with that, she went back into the diner.

As she entered the restaurant, she was met with questioning gazes from everyone in the room. The scene that had just happened would be all over town by the morning. But she wasn't going to worry about gossip or rumors anymore. She didn't have to explain herself to anyone—except possibly her father, who was now standing with Brenda at the counter. They both looked more than a little concerned.

"Bailey," her father said. "Do I need to have a talk with that man?"

"No, Dad. He's gone."

"Good," Brenda said. "I didn't like him at all."

"Neither did I," her father echoed.

She smiled at the fierce protective love and loyalty in their eyes. "I don't like him anymore, either. And I told him that. He won't be back. We're done. I have moved on."

"Maybe you should go tell Ryder that," Brenda suggested.

"Take him his burger," her dad said, handing her a white bag. "Yours is in there, too, as well as some chili fries."

"You guys are the best." She paused. "Ryder is a good guy, too."

"Then you better talk to him, put some light on the situation," her dad said. "Misunderstandings have a way of growing in the dark and in the silence. Believe me, I know." A shadow passed through his eyes.

She wondered if he was talking about the end of his marriage with her mother, but that was a conversation for another day.

———— ❦ ————

When she got to Ryder's house, she was happy to see his Jeep in his driveway. She really hadn't wanted to drive all around town looking for him. But when he opened the door to her persistent knocking, he did not look happy to see her standing on his porch.

"I brought our burgers." She held up the bag in her hand, giving him a tentative smile. "Dad put in chili fries. They're the best."

His frown deepened. "I'm not hungry, and I don't feel like talking."

"Well, I am hungry, and I do feel like talking. I'm not leaving without a conversation."

"You didn't seem to want to talk at the diner, when that slimy weasel told you he loved you and wanted you back."

"Let me explain."

"I don't want an explanation. I saw what I saw."

"You didn't see anything. Let me in, Ryder."

"Damn, you're stubborn."

"So are you," she returned.

"Fine, come in." He turned around and walked away.

She entered the house and moved across the living room to set the bag of food on the coffee table, the big couch reminding her of how much fun they'd had only the night before. *How had things changed so fast?*

Actually, she knew how—first her grandfather

and then Franco.

She turned to face Ryder, who was standing with his arms folded in front of his chest, a hard look in his eyes. "I told Franco I didn't want him back and I didn't want his restaurant," she said. "If you'd stuck around, you would have heard that."

"I heard enough."

"Obviously you didn't."

"He told you he loved you, and you did not say that you didn't love him. You just stood there."

"He took me by surprise," she defended. "But I did tell him exactly that after you left. I made it very clear that I want nothing from him. Whatever we had is over and done."

"Are you sure it's over and done? What about the fact that he told the world you weren't to blame for the food poisoning at his restaurant? When you think about all he can offer you professionally, maybe you'll change your mind about what he has to offer."

"Do you really think I'm that swayed by ambition, Ryder?"

"You said you were before," he reminded her.

"I've learned from my mistakes, and you're the one who told me to stop letting those mistakes hurt me, to look forward, not back. So, why are you trying to drag me into the past?"

"Because your past came into the diner."

"I had nothing to do with that. I certainly didn't invite him."

Ryder drew in a breath and let it out, conflict still running through his eyes. "I didn't like what he said to you, Bailey. I didn't like the way he looked at you. I didn't like him at all."

"Then we shouldn't be arguing, because I feel the

same way. I might not have thrown his flowers in his face, but I did tell him how I felt. I'm glad he came clean to the magazine, that he took responsibility, but I have no interest in having a personal or professional relationship with him. I don't want to hear from him or see him again."

"Even if it hurts your career?"

"Even then. My career is mine. I've finally realized that. It's up to me to make it what I want. No more depending on other people for a leg up or a handout." She took a breath. "So, can we forget about Franco and have lunch?"

"I would like to forget about him," he admitted, as the tension between them slipped away.

"Then I'll heat up our food." She grabbed the bag and headed into the kitchen.

Ryder followed her into the next room, standing in the doorway while she put the burgers and fries in the oven for a few minutes.

"I'm sorry, Bailey. I know that's the second time I've had to apologize today."

His words washed through her with warm relief. "I'm sorry, too, Ryder. I should have reacted more quickly to Franco's declaration. I was just stunned to see him. I could not believe he came all the way to Eagle's Ridge."

"He realized how much you meant to him."

"Probably more like how much work I did for him."

"Will your rejection of him cause you more harm in your restaurant world? Can he hurt you again?"

She was touched that Ryder was worried about that. "He can't hurt me again, and I don't need him to succeed. I never did. I just thought I did."

He nodded. "I'm glad."

"I actually feel good. I feel free. He was a cloud hanging over my head, and now the cloud is gone. It's nothing but blue skies ahead." She laughed as the sound of rain on the window made a mockery of her words. "Well, maybe those blue skies are metaphorical, but you know what I mean."

He smiled. "I know exactly what you mean."

"And," she said, "I know you're unhappy about the way things went with my grandfather. You have a lot on the line." She walked across the room and wrapped her arms around his neck. "But it's still not a hard no…so, we can't give up."

"I like the sound of that *we*," he said huskily.

"So do I," she said, as they came together in a sweet, tender kiss that would have swept them away if the smell of onions hadn't reminded them both that their food was ready. "Let's eat. Then we'll talk or do whatever…"

He smiled for the first time since she'd arrived. "Whatever sounds really good."

"I think so, too."

Fifteen

—➤➤◄◄◄—

After making up with Ryder in the most wonderful way Sunday afternoon, Bailey went home to get some actual sleep and then spent most of Monday working at the diner. When she wasn't at work, she was going through Veronica Westbrook's memory bin.

She spent Monday evening planning her menu for John Westbrook's dinner party on Tuesday, and while Ryder had tempted her with an invitation to dinner, she decided to put business before pleasure, because she really did want to do a good job on the party.

Leasing Veronica's and turning it into her own restaurant was becoming a much more vivid and exciting dream. There were other buildings in town she might be able to convert into restaurant space, but none that offered an architecturally beautiful stone building or such a magnificent view of the river and the mountains. It had to be Veronica's. Her dream was there; she just knew it. Unfortunately, she might have as much chance of convincing John Westbrook to allow her to lease the restaurant as Ryder had with her grandfather, but she was going to take this opportunity to make a good case for her talent as a chef.

Tuesday morning, after taking the day off work at the diner, she got up early and drove an hour out of town to buy fresh produce from a local farmer, then she hit up the Eagle's Ridge markets for her other ingredients. She was going to make a four-course dinner for the Westbrooks, and it had to knock their socks off.

At two o'clock, Ryder picked her up and drove her to his grandfather's house.

As she got out of the Jeep, she was a bit amazed by the sheer magnificence of the home and was reminded once again that she and Ryder had grown up on very different sides of the river.

"It's beautiful," she said. "Sometimes I forget how much wealth your family has."

"It goes back many generations."

"I can't imagine living in a house so big. How many rooms are there?"

"About a dozen. There are six bedrooms and seven baths, plus formal living and dining rooms, a den, an upstairs family room, the kitchen, and some other random bonus rooms."

"It seems a little big for the size of your family."

"It is big. But the Westbrooks like space. It makes not talking to each other a lot easier." He took two grocery bags out of the back of the jeep and handed them to her, then grabbed the rest of the bags. "We'll go in through the kitchen."

"I have to admit I'm feeling nervous, Ryder. I'm sure your grandfather has had some of the best chefs in the world cook for him."

He gave her a reassuring smile as they walked down the drive. "Just do what you do, Bailey. It will be perfect."

"It has to be—for a lot of reasons."

"I know, but I wouldn't have asked you if I didn't believe in you."

"So, where is your mom?"

"She's having a spa day, my gift to her and my aunt. Those would be the two people most likely to get in your way. They're going to be tied up for the next few hours with massages, facials, manicures, and pedicures."

"That sounds great but that can't possibly last until dinner. What happens when your mother gets back? I don't want her to kick me out of the kitchen."

"She won't. I'm picking her up from the spa, and I'll do my best to keep her out of your way. But even if she figures out you're the chef before dinner, it will be too late for her to do anything about it. She won't risk Grandfather's birthday dinner by sending away the only chef we have."

He was probably right, but she'd prefer not to deal with his mother at all.

"By the way, have you heard from your grandfather?" Ryder asked.

"No, I'm sorry." She gave him an apologetic look. "I was so busy yesterday with menu planning and working; I didn't get a chance to talk to him."

"It's fine. He said he was thinking about it. I guess no answer is better than a negative one."

"We'll get an answer tomorrow." She really didn't know what her grandfather was going to do. But they'd made as good of a case as they could.

As Ryder juggled the bags in his hands to open the back door, a crack of thunder rocked the air. She looked up overhead as the day's earlier swirling clouds grew dark and more ominous. A flash of lightning lit up the sky, and rain began to fall as they made their way into a mud room off the kitchen.

"I hope the storm isn't a bad sign of things to come," she muttered.

"There are no bad signs, and everything is going to go well today," he returned.

She was normally quite confident when it came to cooking, but today her nerves tightened and tingled as she walked into the kitchen. The sheer size of it took her breath away. Everywhere she looked, she saw marble-covered counter space with shiny appliances, glass-paned cabinets revealing stemware and china, a double oven and a stove with twelve burners, along with an enormous refrigerator.

She spun around in delight. "This is amazing."

Ryder laughed. "You look like a kid in a candy store."

"I feel that way. This kitchen is as nice as any gourmet restaurant I've worked in." She paused as the door opened and a woman came into the room.

She was older, short, and petite, with straight dark hair to her shoulders, almond-shaped dark eyes, and a friendly smile.

"Hello," she said. "I'm Leticia."

"Bailey Tucker."

"It's nice to meet you. I hope you have everything you need here."

"I can't imagine that I wouldn't. This kitchen is beautiful."

"Far bigger and more sophisticated than I've ever required," Leticia said. "Feel free to use whatever you like. I won't get in your way, but I will be around if you have questions or need help."

"Thanks. I have two servers coming at five. I told them to come around to the kitchen door." She'd asked her dad for some names of people who might be willing to help serve dinner and was thrilled that they'd been available for the party.

"That's fine."

"Where's Grandfather?" Ryder asked.

"He's taking his afternoon nap," Leticia replied. "And your father is at the office. No one should bother Bailey for now, but I make no guarantees for when your mother gets home."

"I'm picking her up from the spa at five," he said. "I'm going to stall her as long as I can."

"Good luck," Leticia said with a smile. "To both of you. I'll be back to check on you, Bailey."

As Leticia left, Ryder moved across the room and slid his arms around her waist. "Do you want me to stay and help you? I've proved I can chop vegetables."

His touch was already stirring her senses, which meant there was only one answer to that question. "No, thanks. You are way too big of a distraction. I need to concentrate."

He gave her a quick, teasing kiss. "Fine, but I missed you last night."

"You've seen me almost every day."

"And yet it isn't enough."

Remarkably, she felt exactly the same way.

He kissed her again, and this time he lingered, his mouth steamy and hot, and she wanted to take a minute to just melt into all that delicious warmth. But she forced herself to push him away. "Go, Ryder. Let me cook. I have a lot to do."

"What are you making?"

"All of your grandfather's favorites from the

restaurants he went to in Paris with Veronica, some of which appeared on her menu, but I'm adding my own spin. I'm going to start the meal with a potato leek soup, followed by a roasted beet and orange salad. For the main course, I'm doing an herb crusted lamb with grapes, bitter lettuces, a chestnut confiture and black walnut jus. With the lamb, I'll be serving a couscous salad with cucumber and red onion and some roasted Brussels sprouts. For dessert, I have the trickiest dish of all, a chocolate soufflé."

"Wow. I'm impressed."

"Wait until I pull it off. Then be impressed."

"It's going to be delicious."

She liked the confidence he had in her. "I hope so."

"I'll see you later."

As Ryder left, she unpacked her grocery bags and got to work.

"I don't know why you have to drive a Jeep," his mother complained as Ryder drove her home from the spa. "It's so—ugly."

"I like it."

He glanced over at her, seeing tension in her face despite the past few hours of pampering. "I thought you'd be more relaxed after your day."

She let out a sigh. "I'm worried about the party and this mystery chef of yours."

"You don't have to worry, and you also don't need to go into the kitchen," he added, as he pulled up in front of the house and parked the Jeep in the drive. "Can you just relax, get dressed, be the hostess, and let my chef handle everything else?"

"I don't know."

"Please, Mom. I need you to trust that I won't let you down."

"I know what's happening, Ryder."

"What do you know?" he asked carefully.

"It's that Tucker girl. She's cooking, isn't she?"

He hadn't expected his mother to guess so accurately. On the other hand, he and Bailey had made quite a scene at No Man's Land on Sunday. There was no doubt there were rumors going around about them. "Yes," he said, choosing not to tell her a lie. At this point, he had to hope she'd let things ride.

"I knew it. Catherine said that you're dating her and that she was probably the chef you'd hired. But I didn't think you'd bring her into your grandfather's house." His mother shook her head, clearly upset. "If your grandfather finds out, he won't even come down for dinner. What possessed you to do this?"

"I want to end the feud between our families."

"On John's birthday?"

"What better day to start over?"

"I can think of 364 other days. Or maybe you just wait a few years. John is an old man. Why do you want to make him unhappy now?"

"I don't want to make him unhappy. I want him to let go of the hatred in his heart for people he doesn't even know."

"We know the Tuckers; it's not just John and Max who had problems. Sam and your father dusted things up a few times. And your aunt and uncle—they've had their problems with the Tuckers, too."

"Like what?"

"I don't know off the top of my head."

"Is that because maybe some of the problems are exaggerated, part of our family lore?"

"Look, I know you want the runway land, but I don't see how Bailey cooking for your grandfather is going to change anything with that. And I doubt Max would want her in our house any more than John does."

"Well, I want her there."

She stared back at him. "So, you are involved with her."

"I am. And I don't care what her last name is. She's a beautiful, intelligent, capable woman and a brilliant chef, and I want you to see that about her."

"How can I see that when I'm not allowed in the kitchen?" she asked tartly.

"You can meet her after dinner."

"Then this is all about us meeting her?"

"Not completely," he admitted. "I want Grandfather to lease Veronica's to Bailey so she can start her own restaurant there."

His mother's jaw dropped. "My goodness, Ryder. You are full of ideas, and they're all bad."

"You can't say I'm not consistent," he said lightly.

"It's not funny. Why do you have to shake everything up? Things are good the way they are."

"Are they good?" he challenged. "We've barely spoken since I got home and I've had even fewer conversations with Dad, who seems to be traveling a great deal of the time."

"Your father and I are fine. He has business elsewhere. And you've been busy; so have I. Founders' Day weekend is always a crazy time."

"It's not this time. It's always. You and I haven't had a relationship since Charlie died."

Her face paled. "How dare you bring up his name?" She put her hand on the door. "I am not having this conversation."

"Stop," he said forcefully. "We have to have this conversation or we're never going to break down this wall between us."

"There's no wall. I don't know what you're talking about."

"I'm talking about being the one who had to be everything his brother couldn't be, and it still wasn't enough. I couldn't make you happy. I couldn't put the smile back on your face, and when I joined the Navy, you couldn't even say good-bye."

"I didn't want you to join the Navy. I didn't want anything to happen to you."

"You never seemed to worry. I barely heard from you."

"I didn't want to know what you were doing. It was easier. If I didn't know where you were, I couldn't worry. I couldn't think about the possibility that I would lose another son. It was too hard."

It was the most honest and revealing statement she'd ever said to him.

"I loved Charlie, too," he said quietly. "I wish he hadn't died. I wish you hadn't had to go through that pain. I wish I could have made it better."

She blinked back tears that seemed to shock her as much as they did him. He couldn't remember seeing her cry, not since the day they'd buried Charlie.

"I—I," she stumbled. "I'm sorry. I know I wasn't the best mother in the world. But you didn't need me. You did good without me. You were smart and strong and successful in everything you did."

"I   knew   you   couldn't   take   any   more

disappointment."

She swallowed hard. "Why are we talking about this now?"

"Because it's why I came home. My helo was shot down, and I didn't know if I'd survive the crash or what waited below, and the strangest things came into my mind in those brief seconds of uncertainty."

"What kind of things?"

"Home. You. Dad. Grandfather, this town. I had always avoided coming back here. I thought I was done with Eagle's Ridge. I'd given up on having a family who could actually talk to each other. But I found myself wanting another chance. When it came time to re-up, I decided not to. I needed to come home. Unfortunately, it's taken me this long to get up the courage to speak to you. You're not an easy person to approach. You have a lot of armor on. But life is short. I knew I had to take one more shot at bringing my family back together."

She stared at him with dark, confused, sad, helpless eyes. "Oh, Ryder, I don't know what to say. I guess I do have armor on. But it wasn't meant to keep you away; it was just meant to protect what was left of my heart after…"

"You can say his name, Mom."

"I really can't," she breathed.

"Okay, you don't have to. You don't have to say anything."

"I've never been good at talking about things that bother me."

"I know."

"I'm sorry I hurt you. You're my son. I love you."

He couldn't remember when or if she'd ever actually told him that before. "I love you, too," he said, feeling a weight lift off his shoulders.

"I'm glad you came back. I'm also glad I didn't know about the crash."

"That's why I didn't tell you until now."

"We'll keep talking," she said. "But not tonight. The family will be coming over, and it's your grandfather's birthday."

"I understand."

"I do have one more thing to say, though."

"What's that?"

"This dinner better be magnificent."

"Bailey won't let us down."

His mother shook her head in bewilderment. "You couldn't find anyone else in this town to like? It has to be her?"

"I'm afraid it does."

"Is she even staying here? I thought she lived in New York?"

"She did, but she'd like to stay." As he said the words, he really hoped they were true. But everything had been happening so fast.

Was Bailey's interest in Veronica's restaurant just an impulsive choice after the problems she'd faced in New York? Would she really be happy running a restaurant in a small town after studying cooking in Paris, Italy, and Spain?

He frowned as he followed his mother into the house, wishing he didn't have any doubts, but he couldn't deny that they were there. He was just going to do what his mother always did when something bothered her—he wasn't going to think about it. The future would come soon enough.

Sixteen

After watching his mother head up to her room, Ryder went into the kitchen where Bailey was whipping a knife through an onion. Her cheeks were red, her eyes a bright blue, and she looked a bit stressed.

"I can't talk to you," she said, then paused, giving him a questioning look. "Unless you've come to tell me your mother is firing me?"

"No, she's not firing you. She knows you're cooking and dinner is a go."

"You told her?"

"She guessed. My aunt said she heard we were seeing each other, and my mom put two and two together."

"And she's okay with it?"

"Okay might not be the right word, but she's going to let you do your thing, so you don't have to worry." He paused. "I also talked to her about Charlie."

Bailey put down the knife, as she looked at him in surprise. "How did that go?"

"Better than I thought. She didn't want to talk at first, but we had a few good moments. It's a small chip in the ice between us."

"It sounds bigger than a small chip. I'm really happy for you, Ryder."

He felt good that he'd finally decided to force the conversation. "I don't know why it took me so long to talk to her."

"It doesn't matter why. You did it, and it was a good thing."

"We'll see. She opened up a little, but she might have slammed that door shut before she got up to her bedroom." As he inhaled, his stomach rumbled. "It smells good in here."

"I hope it tastes as good. Everything is pretty much on track. The servers will be getting here soon. Dinner should be ready right at seven."

"Great. I'm going to change. My mother insists we dress for these kinds of parties."

"Like suit and tie?"

"Exactly."

"I'd like to see you all dressed up," she said with a smile. "Not that I don't like it when you're undressed."

"Okay, now I have to kiss you. Don't stab me," he said, leaning across the counter to take a taste of her soft lips. "Hmm…you've been tasting the food—garlic, onion, some other herb?"

"A lot of other herbs." She pushed him away with a bit of a flustered smile. He liked her flustered, and he had plans to make her a lot more so later on that night.

"Shoo," she said. "I have to work."

"I'm going." He headed out of the kitchen and up the stairs to find a place to change.

After a quick shower, he put on his suit and tie and then joined his family in the living room, deciding not to bother Bailey anymore. She knew what she was doing, and he had to just let her do it.

"You look good, Ryder," his Aunt Catherine said, giving him a hug.

"So, do you," he returned, noting her sleek black dress and perfectly made-up face that took at least ten years off her age.

"How could I not after the wonderful day you treated your mother and me to?"

"I'm glad you enjoyed it."

As he moved past his aunt, he greeted his uncle Thomas and his great-aunt Margaret, his grandfather's younger sister. His dad offered to make him a vodka tonic which he gratefully accepted. *Family parties always went better with a little vodka.*

His mother seemed to be almost through her first or second glass of wine, and she gave him a nervous, wary look, as if afraid of what he would say next. But she didn't have to worry. Tonight was all about his grandfather.

"Happy birthday," he said, shaking John's hand.

"Thank you, Ryder. I hear you spoke to Max the other day. Is he going to sell you his land?"

"He hasn't given me an answer. Who did you speak to?"

"David. He still rates your chances about ninety to ten."

"Glad to know, I have a ten percent chance," he said evenly.

"Those were David's words, not mine," John said sharply.

He took a sip of his drink, surprised when the

doorbell rang. He'd thought all family was present and accounted for. Then Leticia ushered his cousin Ford into the room. With dark hair and dark eyes, Ford definitely looked like both a Garrison and a Westbrook. After Charlie had died, he and Ford had been more like brothers than cousins, despite the fact that Ford was a few years younger.

"Oh, my," Catherine said, rushing over to give her son a hug. "I didn't think you were coming, Ford."

"Your guilt trip worked, Mom," Ford said dryly, greeting the rest of the family with a smile, finally making his way over to Ryder. "Man, it's good to see you, Ryder." He gave him a hug and a slap on the back. "It's been too damn long."

"I'll say. I'm glad you decided to come."

"I've been getting a lot of family pressure."

"How's life in Virginia? How's business?"

"Business is booming and life is good."

"Glad to hear it. I just wish you were a little closer."

"I'm close enough. I didn't expect you to come back to Eagle's Ridge, Ryder. In fact, I didn't think you'd ever leave the Navy."

"It has been a good change for me."

"My mother says you're revamping the airport. I'm happy to hear that. I'm tired of the puddle jumpers that only fly in a few times a day."

"Hopefully, that will change soon." He paused as Leticia came into the room to ask them to be seated in the dining room. "Showtime," he muttered.

Ford raised an eyebrow at his comment. "Is there going to be a show? I thought this was just the usual family dinner."

"It's going to be a dinner you won't forget," he

said.

"In a good way or a bad way?" Ford asked.

He smiled. "Let's find out."

—➤➤◀◀◆—

Bailey had cooked for important people in New York and in Paris, but she'd never felt as stressed as she did tonight. As the servers took out the entrée, she took a minute to wipe some moisture from her face.

She'd done everything she could to plan a menu that Ryder's grandfather would love. So far, through the soup and the salad, the plates had come back completely clean and the servers had told her that everyone was really enjoying the meal.

She thought the lamb was perfectly cooked, the side dishes providing exactly the right accompanying notes. And now she had one more dish to go—the chocolate soufflé. Glancing at the clock, she made a note of the time. She had twenty minutes to go until the soufflé was done. That should give the group enough time to make their way through their entrée and to have the servers clear the plates.

Then it would be time for the ultimate bit of decadence. Walking across the room to her bag, she pulled out a faded and yellow menu from the Parisian restaurant where Veronica had written about the first chocolate soufflé she'd ever tasted on their last night in Paris and how that bit of chocolate heaven had been the perfect way to end their honeymoon and start their lives together.

Reading Veronica's handwriting made her feel close to a woman she'd never met and had little recollection of even seeing from afar. But she felt like she knew her now after having gone through her bin of memories, most of which had to do with food and Paris, and most of which had resonated deeply within her.

She was exactly the right person to take over Veronica's, because while she might not understand the Westbrook way, she did understand Veronica. She just wished Veronica was still alive, that she could have spoken to her about her life, her love of French cooking, even her love of John Westbrook, because there was a Westbrook man in Bailey's heart now, too.

Walking over to the ovens, she stared at the soufflés, seeing the rise in the oven light, hoping they would not turn this amazing dinner into a disaster. She could have gone with a less troublesome dessert, one that might not flop at the very last second, but after having read Veronica's words, she'd known it had to be the soufflé. It was a risk, but one she had to take.

She took the next few minutes to clear away some space on the counters—space which was promptly filled again with dinner plates.

The female server, Paula, gave her a big smile. "Everyone is raving about the lamb," she said. "I've never seen so many happy diners. Rob and I are pouring coffee and tea now. How long until dessert?"

"Five minutes," she said, checking the ovens again.

"Got it."

As Paula went back into the dining room, she paced around the kitchen until the minutes finally ticked off on the clock. The servers came back into the kitchen, along with Leticia, who had been helping out throughout the service and the three of them stood back as she carefully took the first pan out of the oven.

She held her breath as she put each small soufflé dish on a plate. There was absolute and utter quiet from the other three people in the room as she finished off the soufflé with a dusting of sugar.

Finally, the servings were ready to be taken into the dining room. They each picked up two plates and for the first time that evening, Bailey left the kitchen. She wanted to serve all eight desserts at the exact same moment, which needed the four of them to make that happen. She would be blowing her cover as the secret chef, but it couldn't be helped, and it was the perfect time.

As they walked into the dining room, her gaze linked with Ryder's. He gave her a big smile, and that gave her the confidence she needed to take the last few steps.

She put one soufflé down in front of Ryder's mother, who looked more worried than happy when she saw her, and the second one went in front of John Westbrook.

She waited for him to look at her, to recognize her, to call her out, but none of that happened.

His gaze was on the soufflé in front of him. His weathered, old face seemed to lose its color. In fact, he almost seemed to shrink in front of her. She heard him suck in some air, and she suddenly worried that he was in some actual physical discomfort.

"Grandfather," Ryder said. "Are you all right?"

"Chocolate soufflé," John muttered, a bemused note in his voice.

"It looks good," Ryder said.

She probably should have left the table and gone back to the kitchen with the servers and with Leticia, but she couldn't seem to pull herself away. While everyone at the dinner party seemed to realize there was something going on that they didn't understand, no one said a word or started to eat their dessert. All gazes were on John.

He finally picked up his spoon with shaky fingers and dipped it into the middle of the chocolate soufflé.

Bailey held her breath as he pulled out a chunk of the soufflé, happy to see it was the perfect texture.

John put the bite into his mouth and then swallowed. Setting down his spoon, he finally lifted his head and looked at her.

There were shadows in his dark eyes—pain and sadness and yet also the hint of pleasure…or was she just imagining that?

"You're the chef?" he asked.

"Yes," she said.

"The meal took me back to my honeymoon in Paris. The dishes—they were all familiar to me."

"Because you shared them with Veronica," she said softly.

"How did you know?" he asked in confusion.

"Veronica made notes on restaurant menus and postcards about your time there. She said the chocolate soufflé was the perfect ending to your honeymoon and the perfect start to your life together. I thought it would be good for tonight, better than a birthday cake and hopefully just as delicious."

His face tightened, his lips drawing into a taut line, and she could see he was struggling with his emotions—feelings most people probably didn't think John Westbrook had.

"I'll leave you all to your dessert," she said.

"Wait," John said, as she started to leave.

She turned around, afraid she'd left her escape too late.

"Who are you?" he asked.

She thought she heard Ryder's mother make a quick gasp, but she couldn't look away from John Westbrook's commanding gaze. She squared her shoulders and lifted her chin. "I'm Bailey Tucker."

His jaw dropped. "Tucker," he echoed, surprise and dislike in his tone. "You're Max Tucker's granddaughter?"

"I am."

John's gaze moved from her to Ryder. "You set this up? You let a Tucker into my house?"

"Yes. I wanted you to taste Bailey's food, to see how good she is, despite her last name. She's interested in renting Veronica's, opening a new restaurant in that space, one that will do Grandmother's memory proud," Ryder replied evenly.

"What?" John sputtered. "You think I'm going to rent Veronica's to a Tucker?"

"She's amazing chef. You just had one of the best meals of your life, didn't you?"

"I thought it was wonderful," Ryder's mother said unexpectedly.

"I did, too," another younger man at the table said. Bailey was surprised to see Ford Garrison. She hadn't seen Ryder's cousin since high school, but he still looked very much the same with his dark hair and eyes.

After Ford spoke, there was a chorus of approval for the meal she'd just served them.

But John Westbrook was still silent—thoughtful. She didn't know if she should go or stay. Ryder had made a good pitch, but there hadn't been an answer.

She gave Ryder a helpless look.

He frowned and turned back to John. "Don't you agree that the meal was incredible, Grandfather?"

John took another few seconds to put together an answer. "Yes," he said finally. "Thank you."

It wasn't a rave, but she'd take it. "You're welcome. Happy birthday." And with that, she left the dining room.

When she got into the kitchen, she put a hand on the counter and blew out a breath.

Leticia gave her a concerned look. "They know?"

She nodded. "Yes."

"What did John say?"

"It took him awhile, but he said thank you."

Leticia smiled. "That's good."

"I'm not sure if it was good, but at least he didn't throw the soufflé at me."

"He has more bark than bite," Leticia said. "The man feels more deeply than anyone would expect."

As Leticia went back into the dining room to help clear the plates, Bailey thought about Leticia's words. She had seen emotion in John's eyes tonight. John Westbrook might hate the Tuckers, but he'd loved his wife, and tonight a Tucker had given him a taste of an old memory. Maybe that taste had turned a little sour when he realized she'd done the cooking and wanted Veronica's restaurant, or maybe as Ryder hoped, John would finally realize that carrying an old feud through the next several generations was completely pointless.

But whatever was going to happen probably wouldn't happen too fast. It had taken John forever just to say thank you. She felt a little like Ryder had felt when he'd spoken to her grandfather—that while both men might be softening just a little, they were still a long way from saying yes to anything that involved the other family.

The door to the kitchen opened, and Ryder and Ford came into the room.

"That was incredible," Ryder said, giving her a hug and a kiss.

"Thanks," she said, with a breathless smile.

"Do you know Ford?" Ryder asked.

"I remember you from high school. You're Ryder's cousin," she said.

"And you're Adam and Zane's little sister," Ford returned. "I couldn't quite believe it when you showed up in the dining room. A Tucker in the Westbrook house? That was some drama."

"It was Ryder's idea."

"And it was a good one," Ryder put in.

"I think that's still to be seen. I hope my presence didn't spoil your grandfather's birthday."

"It didn't. He finished every last bite of his soufflé, and now he's in the living room, sitting by the fire with everyone. Seriously, Bailey, every single course was perfect."

She beamed at him. "I tried really hard."

"You didn't try; you succeeded."

"I agree," Ford said. "You're an excellent chef, and I'd love to see Veronica's reopened."

"Thanks, but even if John liked the meal, I'm afraid he just won't be able to get past my last name. But I've done all I can do. The rest is up to him." She wearily tucked a strand of hair behind her ear. She was suddenly exhausted. "I better clean up. You two should go back to the party."

"We have everything under control," Leticia interrupted. "You don't need to do anything more,

Bailey."

"Don't be silly. I always finish the job to the very end." She looked back at Ford. "Will you be in town for Founders' Day weekend?"

"I don't know if I'll be here that long," he said. "I may take off tomorrow."

"That soon? Why such a quick visit?" Ryder asked.

"I like seeing Eagle's Ridge and my family for short visits," Ford said. "No time for too much drama." He glanced at Bailey. "How are Adam and Zane these days?"

"They're great. They're getting ready for the spring season. They'll be sorry they missed you; they're in Seattle for a few days for a trade show. They'll be back tomorrow night. If you decide to stay longer, you should give them a call."

"I'll catch them the next time," Ford replied. "I'm going to head back to the living room. It was nice to see you again, Bailey."

"You, too."

"I'll be right there," Ryder told Ford. Then he turned to her, and put his hands on her waist. "Can I say I'm impressed now?"

"You can," she said, as he took another quick kiss. "But you should go back to the party."

"I want to see you later."

She wanted to see him, too, because every time his mouth touched hers, she wanted more. But she was also exhausted. "I'm really tired, Ryder. I'm going to go home and crash. And you should spend tonight with your family—with Ford."

"You could go to my place and crash."

"Tempting, but I wouldn't be much fun."

"You're always fun, but it doesn't always have to be about that," he said, a serious note in his voice. "I just like being with you."

"I like it, too," she murmured, aware that they were not alone in the kitchen, even though she was barely conscious of the activity going on around her. "But tonight has been—a lot. I feel like I put all my cards on the table, but I still don't know if I won, if it will be enough."

"I understand how you feel. I felt that way after I spoke with your grandfather."

"I understand your mood from the other day a lot better now." She gave him a smile, but he didn't return it. She could see there was something else going on in his head now. "What?"

"I was just thinking…"

"About?"

"It doesn't matter. We'll talk later."

"Tomorrow," she agreed.

He kissed her again and left the kitchen.

Clean-up, then bed, she told herself. She didn't want to think or worry or plan anymore. She just wanted to rest. Tomorrow would be here soon enough.

———

Ryder paused in the hall outside the kitchen door. He could hear family conversation coming from the living room, but he wasn't ready to join them yet. Bailey's recent words had made him think about things in a different way—and it wasn't a particularly good way.

She'd told him that she wanted her own restaurant, that she knew it for certain now.

What if his grandfather wouldn't let her lease Veronica's? Would she be able to find a place in town that suited her needs?

Even if she did, would it be right for her?

He'd just seen Bailey shine in a way he'd never really imagined. She wasn't just a good chef; she was an incredible chef. She had talent beyond talent. Was she really going to be happy cooking in a small town like Eagle's Ridge? She could be anywhere in the world—New York, Paris, London, Rome—places she'd already told him she'd been and loved. Her dreams had taken her far from home. And they hadn't really brought her back now.

She'd come home to Eagle's Ridge because it was a safe haven, a place to be comforted and nurtured, to be with family and old friends.

Was it really where she was meant to stay?

And if it wasn't, would he have to let her go?

Seventeen

Bailey woke up early Wednesday morning, the force of the wind and the pounding rain waking her from her deep, exhausted sleep. It was almost seven but dark as midnight. Throwing on her robe and slippers, she went down the stairs and into the living room. Her dad was in the kitchen and on the phone with someone. As she drew nearer, she could hear the tension in his voice.

"I'll be right there," he said. "Thanks for letting me know."

"What's wrong?" she asked, as he hung up the phone.

"One of the front windows blew out at the diner. Chuck Hayes was driving by and saw the glass on the street."

"I'll get dressed," she said quickly.

"I can't wait for you, Bailey."

"Of course not. I'll be there as soon as I can. I hope there's not a lot of damage."

"Me, too," he said grimly. "I'm also worried about your grandfather. I heard the river is coming over the road. I was about to head up there when Chuck called."

She met his troubled gaze and remembered how high the river had been near her grandfather's house on Sunday. "I'll check on him as soon as I get dressed."

"Bring him back here," her dad said. "He won't want to come, but you need to convince him."

"I will." That promise might be a little difficult to keep, but she'd give it her best shot.

After her dad left, she jogged back to her room and threw on her clothes, taking just a minute to brush her teeth and pull her hair into a ponytail, and then she headed out the door.

The wind and rain swamped her with a fierce fury that was much stronger than she'd expected. She had to battle just to get to her car.

She drove down the road, her worry increasing as branches flew off the trees, hitting her windows with almost breaking force. She was a quarter-mile from her grandfather's house when she found herself driving through inches of water, and it was getting deeper by the minute.

Her grandfather's house sat lower along this part of the river than her dad's house, and it was clear that the flooding was only going to get worse. She pulled up about twenty yards from the house, afraid to go much farther and jumped out.

The water was up to her ankles, and she was glad for the knee-high rain boots she'd put on over her jeans. She slogged through the water to her grandfather's steps, then ran up to the front door and rang the bell sharply three times. Her grandfather might still be asleep, but she needed to get him out of the house before the road became impassable.

Finally, he opened the door, wearing baggy sweatpants and a sweatshirt, a haggard look on his face. "What the hell?" he swore, bleary-eyed. "What are you doing here, Bailey?"

"The river is flooding the road," she said, stepping into his house. "It's already a foot deep. You need to come to Dad's house with me now."

"I'm not going anywhere. I got a generator, plenty of food and water. It's all good."

"It's not all good. Who knows how high the river will go? It could flood this house if the rain continues like it is."

"It would have to come up another three or four feet."

"It just might do that. Please don't be stubborn about this, Grandpa. Let me take you to Dad's house."

"I am not leaving my home, Bailey. I appreciate your concern, but I have never left before, and I'm not leaving now."

"Why?" she asked in frustration. "It's just a house."

"It's not just a house; it's my life. It's everything I have. But you need to go now. Don't worry about me."

"I can't leave without you."

"Well, you can't stay. You'll get stuck here."

She let out a breath of frustration, wishing her brothers were in town or her dad had come with her. She couldn't forcibly carry her grandfather to her car, but she didn't think there was any other way he was going to go with her.

Max strode to the door and opened it. The gusty wind blew a shower of rain into the entry. "Go now," he ordered.

She walked over to the door and shut it. "I'm not leaving you, Grandpa."

"I don't have enough food and water for both of us, and your dad will want your help at the diner. If the storm gets worse, people will evacuate, and they'll be needing hot food."

"That's true, and I should be there, but if you're staying, I'm staying."

He glared at her. "Don't be disrespectful."

"I'm not. I'm trying to make sure you stay as healthy as you are. I cannot let you get cut off from the world and be out here all by yourself."

A blast of wind hit the house so hard the windows rattled and the door burst open. She heard something that sounded like thunder but soon realized that the house was shaking, that one corner of the ceiling in the living room was shattering.

Her grandfather pushed her behind him as a huge tree came through the roof. Rain, branches and leaves rained down around them.

The shock of the tree, the wind, the rain, and the roof falling in stole her breath away. Finally, she said, "Grandpa, are you all right?" As he turned to face her, she saw blood on his face. "You're bleeding."

He put his fingers to his face. "It's nothing, just a cut."

"Come on, get whatever you need for the next few days, and we'll go to Dad's house."

"I can't leave the house like this. Rain is coming in everywhere."

"You can't stay here now," she said, shocked he was still hesitating.

"I need to cover things up. There are tarps in the basement." He was down the hall and through the basement door before she could stop him. When he came up with the tarps, she could see water dripping off the hems of his sweatpants.

"Is there water in the basement?" she asked.

"Help me," he said, throwing her a tarp.

She followed him back into the living room, noting that he'd avoided answering her question. For the next few minutes, they pulled furniture into the far side of the room, away from where the roof had fallen in, and then covered it with the tarps, anchoring them down with heavy books from the shelves.

"Pack a bag," she said. "We need to go." She walked over to the window and looked outside and suddenly realized it was too late to leave.

The water had risen around her car past the bottom of the doors and the road had to be at least several feet deep.

Her grandfather joined her at the window. "It will be all right, Bailey."

As if to make a mockery of his statement, another heavy branch came through the roof.

"It's not going to be all right. We need help."

"No one can make it down that road," he told her.

"Maybe someone with a boat," she suggested. "But Adam and Zane are out of town, dammit."

"Doesn't matter. No one can get a boat here in this current. It would be too dangerous. We have to wait for the river to go down."

Another tree branch came through the roof and the force shattered a nearby window. More rain sprayed into the room. She was already cold, and it had only been a few minutes. They could not stay here. There had to be a way out.

She took her phone out of her pocket and Ryder's

name popped up first on her list of contacts. Relief ran through her. *Ryder would know what to do.* "I'm calling Ryder."

"I don't need a Westbrook's help."

"Oh, just stop it," she said, moving away from him. "I don't care about your ridiculous feud anymore."

Ryder picked up on the second ring. "Hey, Bailey."

"I'm in trouble," she said shortly.

"What's wrong?"

"I drove out to my grandfather's house to bring him back to my dad's house, but the river has flooded the road. It's several feet deep and the current is running fast. Grandpa doesn't think anyone can get a boat out here, at least not until it stops raining."

"I wouldn't think so. Has the water reached the house?"

"Not yet, but that could happen in the next few hours and that's not even all of it. A tree came through the roof."

"Are you both all right?"

"For now," she said, unable to keep the fear out of her voice. "But we can't stay here, and we can't get out. I really don't know what to do."

"Well, I do, Bailey. I'll come and get you in the helo," he said.

"Can you take it up in this storm?"

There was a slight hesitation on his end, then he said, "It will be fine."

His doubts made her worry even more, not just about her own situation, but about what Ryder now wanted to do. "We can wait until the storm lessens," she said. "You don't have to do it now. Maybe the river will go down when the rain stops."

"I'm going to head to the airport. I'll check the weather and wind conditions, and then I'll come and get you."

Her hand gripped the phone as she was torn apart by conflicting emotions. If she was the only one trapped, she could survive, but she wasn't as sure about her grandfather. He'd sat down on the arm of a chair, and he was dabbing at the blood on his face with a napkin. Despite his tough appearance, he was ninety-three years old, and she didn't know how long he could survive in the cold and the rain.

"I don't want anything to happen to you, Ryder. I don't want you to risk your life for me."

"I know what I'm doing, Bailey. You don't have to worry about me. I'll call you back when I get to the airport. If for some reason, we lose contact, keep an eye out for me."

"Okay," she said. "But please be safe."

"We're both going to be safe."

She really hoped he was right.

"What's going on?" Ford asked Ryder, as he got up from the living room couch where he'd spent the night.

They'd gone to Baldie's after dinner and had thrown back a few drinks, and his cousin had decided to stay at his house rather than go to his parents' home.

"Bailey and her grandfather are stranded at her grandfather's house. A tree came through the roof and the road is impassable. She doesn't know if the river will reach the house, but it's possible. I need to get them."

Ford snapped fully awake at his words. "The storm is raging, Ryder. You can't take the helo up in this."

"I'm going to the airport. I'll wait for a break in the wind and then I'll go."

"With who?" Ford challenged.

"I don't know yet. I'll have to see who I can find. But if no one is available, I have a remote control on the helo. I can operate the bucket by myself."

"That would be incredibly dangerous both for you and for them."

He couldn't disagree, but he also couldn't let anything happen to Bailey.

"I'll come with you," Ford offered.

He immediately shook his head. "I can't let you do that."

"You're not letting me do anything," Ford said. "I'm coming. Don't argue."

He didn't want to risk his cousin's life, but also knew it would be less dangerous to have Ford operate the bucket while he kept the helo steady. With the force of the wind, that wouldn't be easy. "All right. Thanks."

Within minutes, they were dressed and ready for action. The drive to the airport did not give him confidence in being able to take the helo up. The wind was howling, and the rain was still coming down in sheets of water. But the storm also reminded him that Bailey and her grandfather's situation was getting more precarious by the minute.

When they got to the airport, no one was there. They'd cancelled the two flights coming in that day an hour earlier and everyone had gone home. But the helo was sitting on the pad, ready to fly when he could.

For the next hour, he and Ford kept an eye on the weather conditions. He was antsy, eager to get out there and get Bailey, but while he was willing to push the envelope, he had to be smart. If something happened to him, it would make everything worse for her.

"You're in love with her," Ford said with a gleam in his eyes. "Last night you said you cared about her, but this is serious, isn't it?"

"As serious as it gets. I can't lose her, Ford, at least not this way."

"What does that mean?"

"It means I don't know if she should stay in Eagle's Ridge. You tasted her food. She has real talent, talent that should have a bigger stage than this town. I want her to stay, but I don't know if it's the right thing for her."

"It's her decision, Ryder. She gets to choose."

"I know. I just want her to be happy, to have her dreams. They were big enough to take her away from here before."

"Dreams change. What she wanted before may not be what she wants now. You need to talk to her."

"I will—as soon as I get her back safe and sound." He checked the weather again. Finally, the wind speeds had decreased. It looked like they had a small window of time to make their rescue.

He called Bailey, relieved that her phone was still working. "I'm leaving now," he said. "I should be there within ten to fifteen minutes. Can you get out to the deck?"

"Yes. But there are trees all around," she said,

worry in her voice.

"That's okay. I can hang above the tree line."

"Are you sure it's safe?"

"Trust me," he said. "I'm not going to let anything happen to you."

"Don't let anything happen to you, either," she implored.

"I'll see you soon."

Eighteen

"Ryder is coming to get us," she told her grandfather, both relieved and worried there was a plan.

He didn't look happy with her words, but she didn't care. He'd spent the past hour trying to tell her how they could stay in the bedroom until the storm ended, but the entire house was freezing and wet, and her grandfather had already started to cough.

She'd gotten her father on the phone earlier and explained that they were trapped and that Ryder was going to fly in when he could, but she needed her dad to talk her grandfather into leaving. That had ended in a shouting match between the two of them. Then her grandfather had spent the next twenty minutes arguing with her.

"That damn Westbrook fool is going to kill all of us," Max muttered. "Taking a helicopter up in a storm like this is nonsense."

"Ryder is not a fool; he knows what he's doing," she retorted. "You're the one acting like an idiot. Ryder is a brave, courageous man, who is willing to risk his life to come and get us. And his cousin, Ford, is coming, too, another person willing to put his life on the line for two Tuckers. Have you considered that at all?"

"They're coming to get you, not me. Ryder is in love with you. Anyone can see that."

Her heart swelled with her grandfather's words. "I don't know if it's love, but—"

"Now who's being the idiot? And you're in love with him. I can't believe it." He shook his head in amazement. "A Tucker loving a Westbrook—how could this happen? You're going to end up being one of them—my own granddaughter."

"Maybe Ryder will end up being one of us. Why don't you look at it that way? And while we're talking about it, are you going to sell Ryder the land for the runway or not?"

"I'm still thinking."

"No, you're just trying to torture Ryder, and it's not nice. You know that land is worth nothing to you, and our family will benefit as much as Ryder will from the airport expansion. So why don't you stop thinking through the haze of sixty-five years of anger and do what's right?"

He stared back at her. "You've got a mouth on you."

"I've also got brains and heart. And I got them from you, Grandpa. At least, I thought I did. I hope you're going to prove me right."

Before he could answer, she got a text on her phone from Ryder and heard the buzz of a helicopter. "He's here. Let's go out on the deck."

She grabbed the overnight bag she'd insisted her grandfather pack. He'd put in a couple of clothing items as well as scrapbooks, photos and his banking information. She hoped when the storm ended, and they came back to the house, he'd be able to get everything that meant something to him. If many more trees came through the roof, everything could be lost. But right now, it was his life she was concerned about.

When they got onto the deck, she saw the helicopter approaching the house. It was still raining, and the wind was gusting, but it wasn't nearly as bad as it had been.

As the helicopter came overhead, she could see Ryder at the controls and Ford near the open door. A moment later, a large bucket was lowered down.

It blew wildly in the wind, and she was a little terrified that this was their only way out. "I don't know if I can do this," she muttered.

Her grandfather grabbed her hand and gave it a squeeze. "You'll be okay," he told her, reminding her now of the strong man she'd always looked up to.

"I know," she said, drawing in a breath. "You're getting in first, Grandpa."

"You go, then I'll follow."

She shook her head. "You won't follow. You'll go back in the house, and I won't let that happen. I need you, Grandpa. I need you to live." As the basket reached them, she let go of her grandfather and grabbed it. "Get in. And for God's sake, don't argue anymore. The longer this takes, the more danger we'll all be in."

He must have sensed she was at the end of her rope, because he reluctantly got in the bucket. She put the overnight bag in the bucket with him, then gave Ford a thumbs up. She held her breath as the bucket was slowly raised above the trees, and her grandfather was pulled safely into the helicopter. Then it was her turn.

When the basket came down again, it took all her guts to get inside. The ride was as frightening as she'd imagined, and she was about six feet off the ground when the wind suddenly gusted, knocking the bucket into the trees. She ducked her head, holding on tight, terrified that she might get thrown out.

But seconds later, she was moving upward again. The rain came down harder on her head as the basket moved up and over the trees. She closed her eyes, praying they'd all make it.

Finally, Ford was pulling her into the helicopter with a reassuring smile. "It got a little exciting there for a minute."

She tried to smile back but fell woefully short. "Thanks for not dumping me out."

"Ryder wouldn't have liked that," he joked, handing her a blanket.

She wrapped the blanket around her shoulders and sat next to her grandfather, putting her hand in his as Ryder flew them back to the airport.

When they landed, Ford helped her grandfather out of the helicopter and over to Ryder's car, while Ryder gave her a tight hug of relief and a hot kiss that warmed her cold, trembling lips.

"Thank you," she said. "You saved our lives. The water was getting higher by the minute."

He gazed into her eyes. "There's no way I was going to lose you. Come on, let's get you somewhere safe and dry. He put his arm around her and led her to the Jeep.

They dropped Ford at his parents' house, with

more expressions of gratitude for his part in the rescue, and then headed toward her dad's place.

As they went across the bridge, she saw plywood over two of the front windows of the diner, but there were lots of cars in the parking lot. The storm had not dampened business. She pulled out her phone and punched in her dad's number.

"Bailey?" he said, tension in his voice.

"We're safe," she reassured him. "Grandpa and I are on our way to your house. He's fine. I'm fine. It's all good."

"Thank God. I haven't been able to breathe, wondering what was happening."

"How's it going at the diner?"

"Aside from losing a few windows, we're good. I'll be home in a few hours."

"No rush. We're okay." She'd no sooner finished speaking when Ryder parked in front of her father's house.

She helped her grandpa inside and insisted he take a hot shower. While he was doing that, she put his overnight bag in the bedroom that had once belonged to Adam and Zane and was now the official guest room. Then she moved into her bedroom, stripped off her wet clothes, dried her hair, and put on yoga pants and a long sweater.

When she returned to the living room, she saw Ryder in the kitchen and heard the kettle singing.

"Do you want some tea or hot chocolate?" he asked, as she entered the room. "I found both in your father's cupboards."

She walked across the room and wrapped her arms around him, resting her head on his broad shoulder.

He hugged her tight, and they stayed like that for a very long minute. She didn't want to let go of him—not now, not ever. Her grandfather had told her she was in love with Ryder. She didn't know why she hadn't admitted that to herself or to Ryder. This man was everything she had ever wanted and more.

She lifted her head so she could look into his eyes. "I love you, Ryder. And I'm not saying that because you just saved my life and my grandfather's life. It's how I feel—how I've felt since I came back, since you rescued me and Gambler from the river." She smiled at that. "You seem to be making a habit of rescuing me."

His gaze filled with warmth and affection. "I will always rescue you. I love you, too, Bailey. But…"

"There's a *but*?" she asked with alarm.

"But," he repeated. "I don't want to hold you back. Eagle's Ridge is a small town. And you have enormous talent. I saw it last night. You need a stage, a place to shine, to be known, where people can flock to your restaurant and eat your incredible food. I don't know if this town is big enough for you."

She was incredibly touched by his words, by his concern for her and her dreams. "I can create the restaurant of my dreams here. If not at Veronica's, then someplace else."

"Or I can follow you where you want to go."

"You would really do that? Your life is here. You came back to start over with your family, to build a new life, and you've earned it."

He tightened his arms around her waist. "That's true, but didn't I just say I love you? There are no geographic boundaries when it comes to love. And the bottom line is that I'm not going to let you out of my life. If you want New York or Paris or any city in the world, I'm sure I can find something to do, some helicopter to fly. And as for my family, we sometimes do better when we're not too close."

"I can't believe you would consider moving for me. This is happening really fast, Ryder."

"I'm not trying to rush you; I just want you to know where I stand. When I thought about possibly losing you today, I knew that nothing else in my life was more important than you."

She nodded. "I was thinking the same thing. So, kiss me already."

"My pleasure." She wrapped her arms around his neck, and he gave her a long, deep kiss filled with promise, with love, with dreams... And when she lifted her gaze to his, she had not a doubt in her mind what she wanted to do.

"I want to stay here, Ryder. I want to make a life in Eagle's Ridge. I love to travel, but I've lived in the big cities you just mentioned. I've had that life, and it never made me completely happy. I want to cook for people who appreciate my food. I want to have total control over a restaurant and the freedom to experiment. But career aside, I want to be with you, so we'll figure it out, right?"

"Right," he echoed. "I just don't want you to feel like you're giving anything up."

"How could I feel that way when I'm about to get everything I ever wanted?"

"I'm getting everything I ever wanted, too. Now, why don't we take this conversation to my house, so we don't have a chaperone?"

"I like that idea a lot."

"Not so fast," her grandfather interrupted, as he

entered the kitchen, looking a lot better than he had earlier. The color had returned to his face. His forehead had stopped bleeding, and the gash didn't look nearly as bad as it had before. "I have something to say."

Ryder kept his arm around her shoulder, as they turned to face her grandfather, making it clear they were together, but she could feel his tension. She wanted to believe what her grandfather was about to say would be good, maybe an expression of gratitude, a thank you, but she couldn't quite tell from his ominous tone.

"Yes, sir?" Ryder asked.

"I'll sell you the land," her grandfather said. "It won't be cheap."

"I wouldn't expect it to be," Ryder returned.

"But there's a condition."

"Grandpa, please," she protested.

"This is between Westbrook and me," he told her.

"What's the condition?" Ryder asked.

"Don't hurt my granddaughter."

"That's an easy promise to make. I love her."

"Well, any damn fool could see that," her grandfather retorted.

Bailey smiled at Ryder. "I guess we're kind of an item around town."

"I'm not unhappy about that." He gazed back at her grandfather. "Thank you."

"Make it a good runway, a better airport. I want you to do everything you promised me the other day. That runway will be my legacy to this town."

"I understand, and I won't let you down," Ryder said.

The doorbell rang. "I'll get that," Bailey said.

She walked out of the kitchen and into the entry. She threw open the door, not sure who would be on the other side, but she never in a million years expected it to be John Westbrook. As far as she knew, the old man rarely left the house, and he never came to this side of the river.

"Bailey," he said. "I'd like to come in. It's still raining."

"Of course." She waved him inside. "I—what—what are you doing here?"

"I'd like to know the answer to that, too," her grandfather bellowed, as he and Ryder came down the hall.

The four of them stared at each other for a long second, then John said, "I came to see Bailey. I can't believe I had to step into a Tucker house to do it, but I heard she was here when I went to the diner."

"What do you want with Bailey?" Max demanded.

"That's between her and me," John snapped.

She swallowed nervously as John Westbrook's gaze turned to hers. Then he reached into his pocket and pulled out a key on a silver ring and handed it to her.

"What's this?" she asked, her heart racing.

"It's the key to Veronica's. You earned it last night. You reminded me of a wonderful time in my life, a memory that I still cherish."

"I'm glad," she murmured.

He cleared his throat. "I know you probably did it to butter me up. But I also know that Veronica would want you to run her restaurant. She never wanted it to sit empty. I was the one who couldn't bear to see it taken over by someone who would destroy what she'd built, but you understand her. You love what she loved."

"I do," she agreed. "And I promise to honor her memory in the restaurant. I already have an idea for the name of it."

"You do?" Ryder asked curiously.

She nodded as she looked back at his grandfather. "Veronica wrote in her journal that the night she walked with you on the Champs-Élysées under a rare blue moon that she finally knew what love was all about. I'd like to call the restaurant Blue Moon."

John's eyes blurred with moisture, and his jaw tightened. "Veronica would like that. She used to look through the windows of her restaurant in search of that same blue moon, and a few times she saw it. She always said it was a touchstone to her life, a reminder of how lucky she was."

"Not only to have seen the blue moon, but to have found you," she whispered, remembering Veronica's words.

"I always loved her," John said, his gaze swinging to Max. "She was never yours."

Max gave him a hard glare, and for a moment, Bailey thought her grandfather would resort to the same old tired argument that he could have had Veronica if John hadn't stolen her from him. But her grandfather's hesitation was new. And when he opened his mouth this time, so were his words.

"I thought she could have been, but I know that was just an illusion," Max admitted.

"You do?" the three of them in the room said at the same time, creating one long echo.

"I'm not stupid," her grandfather retorted. "Or at least I'm not anymore. I still think you screwed me over with the bet and the land, John. You knew I was in pain the night of that game. You knew I was drunk."

"I did. But I also knew you'd been trying to get Veronica away from me."

"Get her away from you? She wanted to spend time with me."

"As a friend. She only ever loved you as a friend. She told me so."

Max glared at John. "But you couldn't even let her be my friend after you married."

"You were acting crazy back then. You might not remember it, but I do. You were running around town, drinking too much, gambling whenever you could. If you hadn't lost that land to me, you would have lost it to someone. At least I used it to build up the town, to make Eagle's Ridge what it is today. You should have been grateful."

"Grateful?" Max echoed. "I was the one who said we should go hiking in Washington. If we hadn't found Eagle's Ridge together, we never would have come here at all. I bet you forgot about that."

"You may have found the land, but I fronted the money to all of you, so we could buy it together," John declared.

"It's always been about money with you."

"No, it was supposed to be about friendship, but instead we became enemies, and here we are."

"Here we are," Max echoed.

The two men stared at each other for another long, tense minute.

"We're old," John continued, a weary note in his voice.

"You're older than me," Max pointed out.

John sighed. "Can we be done, Max?"

"I can be done, if you can be done. I don't really need to waste any more time thinking about you."

"I agree."

Bailey couldn't quite believe what she was hearing. She glanced at Ryder, who seemed to be just as surprised at the turn of events.

"Does this mean you can both put your feud aside?" Ryder asked.

"Not going to be much of a feud with you two mooning over each other," Max grumbled. "You do know you're going to have a Tucker for a granddaughter-in-law one of these days, don't you, John?"

John nodded. "I had a hunch when I saw them together last night. Looks like it's their time now."

"I can't disagree," Max said. "I'm selling Ryder the land he wants."

"And I'm leasing Bailey the restaurant she wants," John said. "So that's it. The feud is over. Now, I'll be going. Leticia is waiting in the car."

"I'll take a ride to the diner if you've got room," Max said.

"I suppose I do," John said. "Come on then."

Bailey couldn't believe what she was seeing: Max Tucker and John Westbrook not only walking out the door together but also getting into the same car.

"Am I dreaming?" she asked Ryder, as he put his arm around her once again.

"If you are, I am, too."

"How did this happen?"

He turned her to face him. "Our plan worked. We ended the feud. We got the land and the restaurant. I think the two of us make an amazing team."

She laughed at the look of pride in his eyes. "We did do what we set out to do. But I don't think it was our plan that brought them together; I think it was love."

"Uh, I'm not sure if they love each other again. But it looks like they're both ready to make peace."

She gave him a playful slap on the shoulder. "I'm not talking about them; I'm talking about us. Our love brought our families together, and we didn't have to die to make that happen. It's a lot better than Romeo and Juliet."

He grinned. "I totally agree. So, back to my house?"

"It's kind of far away. I think I'd like to show you my bedroom instead."

"Good. Because I can't wait to love you."

"And I can't wait to love you back, Ryder."

Epilogue

—⇒➤➤◄◄◄—

Friday morning was bright and sunny and a perfect day for a parade. *There was a lot to celebrate,* Bailey thought, as she and Ryder joined Zane and Adam and other members of their families in front of the stage that had been set up in front of City Hall.

Today wasn't going to be a singular Founder's Day in honor of John Westbrook but a group Founders' Day celebrating all of the founders: John Westbrook, Max Tucker, David Bennett, and Will Coleman.

The four men were seated in chairs on the makeshift stage while Mayor Warren prepared to welcome the crowd for a kick-off speech that would be followed by a parade and a weekend-long festival of games, art, music, and carnival rides.

"I still can't quite believe they're all together," she said, taking a hold of Ryder's hand. "Miracles really can happen."

"I can't believe it, either," Zane said, drawing her attention to him. "We go to Seattle for a few days and all hell breaks loose. Ryder has to rescue you and

Grandpa, and the old men end sixty-five years of feuding, all because you two are in love."

She laughed at the bemused expression on Zane's face. "Love conquers all. You should try it some time."

"I think not," he returned. "I like being single."

"You better treat Bailey right," Adam put in, giving Ryder a pointed look. "Or you'll answer to us."

"I'm not worried about answering to anyone," Ryder said dryly. "I have every intention of making Bailey very, very happy."

"I like the sound of that," she said, giving his hand a squeeze.

He smiled down at her. "Me, too."

"We are glad you're staying in town, Bailey," Zane interrupted. "Now you can help us with A To Z Watersports."

"I'm going to be opening a restaurant," she reminded him. "I'll be very busy."

"Then Ryder can help," Adam suggested.

"I'm going to be building a runway," Ryder said.

Adam laughed and gave Zane a shrug. "I don't think we're getting any help, Zane."

Zane nodded. "Guess not."

"By the way," Bailey said. "I talked to Mom yesterday. I told her everything that's been going on. She really wants to come home for a visit in the spring. I told her she should come back for the grand opening of Blue Moon, and she liked the idea. I'm giving you guys two months to get used to the idea. I'm planning to open sometime at the end of May."

Adam groaned. "Why did you invite her?"

"Because we ended one old feud; maybe it's time we ended another."

"It's not the same thing," Zane said.

"I know it's not the same, but we're all grown up now. We should be able to see each other at important events. I think it's a good idea."

"She probably won't come, Bailey," Adam said, folding his arms across his chest, an annoyed look in his eyes. "You know how good she is at keeping promises."

"He's right," Zane added. "You've always wanted everything to end happily ever after, Bailey. Sometimes it doesn't."

"But sometimes it does," she said forcefully. "Sometimes the worst moments in life lead to the best ones." She turned to face the man who had stolen her heart. "I am so grateful for everything that happened to me in New York, because if it hadn't, I might not have come home. I might have missed out on us, Ryder."

"I'm glad I made it home, too," Ryder said, gazing deep into her eyes. "I knew there was a reason I had to come back here. I just didn't know it was you."

She gave him a kiss, hearing her brothers groan in unison. Breaking away, she gave Zane and Adam a mischievous smile and, "Get used to it, guys, because I plan on kissing Ryder a lot."

"I've never been so happy to hear the mayor speak," Zane muttered as Mayor Warren stepped up to the microphone.

She laughed. "One day, you two are going to be just as madly in love with someone as I am. And I can't wait for that to happen."

Both Adam and Zane rolled their eyes in perfect twin unison and looked toward the stage.

"I really don't want to hear this speech," Ryder said, giving her a wicked look. "Have we seen enough of Founders' Day yet?"

She glanced at the stage, at the four old men sitting next to each other, and nodded. "I think our work is done here. It's time to get started on the rest of our lives."

"I couldn't agree more."

THE END

Get the complete series:

Ryder – Barbara Freethy (#1)
Adam – Roxanne St. Claire (#2)
Zane – Christie Ridgway (#3)
Wyatt – Lynn Raye Harris (#4)
Jack – Julia London (#5)
Noah – Cristin Harber (#6)
Ford – Samantha Chase (#7)

About The Author

Barbara Freethy is a #1 New York Times Bestselling Author of 64 novels ranging from contemporary romance to romantic suspense and women's fiction. Traditionally published for many years, Barbara opened her own publishing company in 2011 and has since sold over 6.5 million books! Twenty-two of her titles have appeared on the New York Times and USA Today Bestseller Lists. She is a six-time finalist and two-time winner in the Romance Writers of America acclaimed RITA contest.

Known for her emotional and compelling stories of love, family, mystery and romance, Barbara enjoys writing about ordinary people caught up in extraordinary adventures. Romance Reviews Today calls her a "master storyteller". Library Journal says, "Barbara Freethy has a gift for writing unique and compelling characters."

For a complete listing of books, as well as excerpts and contests, and to connect with Barbara:

Visit Barbara's Website:
www.barbarafreethy.com

Join Barbara on Facebook:
www.facebook.com/barbarafreethybooks

Follow Barbara on Twitter:
www.twitter.com/barbarafreethy

Made in the USA
Lexington, KY
22 October 2017